MW01632842

Crossing Morgan's Creek

A Novel by Ben Gill

ALSO BY BEN GILL

The Joy of Giving

Stewardship

Random Thoughts from a Wandering Mind

HOW TO ORDER

Books are available from Amazon.com. Search by name of author or book title. For quantity orders or to request signed copies, please go to www.bengill.com and select the "Books by Ben" link. An order form can be printed and faxed to the appropriate distributor.

Myriad Communications, Inc.,
is an imprint of
Viscern
5151 Belt Line Road, Suite 900
Dallas, TX 75254
Library of Congress Cataloging-in-Publishing Data
ISBN: 0-9642146-2-8
Printed in Belarus

Myriad Communications, Inc., is a registered trademark of Viscern.
Cover design by Ted Dysart, Jr.
Content edited by Ruth Anne Franks.

Dedication

For all the Rev. Earl Lees; the Rev. and Most Holy and Apostolic Moses R. Johnsons; the Bro. Webbs; and most of all the Leroy Everses of the story who influenced my life as a boy in Arkansas.

They are symbolic of the many who crossed my path and whose influences remain a part of my life even until this day.

Acknowledgements

NO LITERARY WORK is the result of one person's efforts. As such, this book is a compilation of many influences in my life.

I am indebted to the people of the Mississippi Delta of northeast Arkansas who influenced my life far more than I ever thought would be the case.

I am indebted to my wife, Holly, who never complained about the all-night writing sessions that were necessary to produce this work.

I am indebted to the team at Viscern who understood my distractions as I sought to meet their deadlines.

I am indebted to Ruth Anne Franks, content editor, who corrected as much of the poor grammar as possible and was especially adept at determining when it was part of the story or when it was simply my poor writing style.

I am indebted to Ted Dysart, Jr., who continues to make covers attractive enough to entice potential readers.

But most of all I am indebted to you, the reader, who will take time from your busy life to allow me to share Sam's life with you. I do hope you enjoy the reading as much as I did the writing.

Amazing Grace

Amazing grace! (how sweet the sound)
That sav'd a wretch like me!
I once was lost, but now am found,
Was blind, but now I see.

'Twas grace that taught my heart to fear,
And grace my fears reliev'd;
How precious did that grace appear,
The hour I first believ'd!

Thro' many dangers, toils and snares,
I have already come;
'Tis grace has brought me safe thus far,
And grace will lead me home.

The Lord has promis'd good to me,
His word my hope secures;
He will my shield and portion be,
As long as life endures

Yes, when this flesh and heart shall fail,
And mortal life shall cease;
I shall possess, within the vail,
A life of joy and peace.

The earth shall soon dissolve like snow,
The sun forbear to shine;
But God, who call'd me here below,
Will be for ever mine.

Words written by John Newton in 1772
Source: The Cowper and Newton Museum
(United Kingdom)

AMEN, AMEN, AND THANK YOU, JESUS!

Preface

LONG BEFORE I PUT HIS STORY on paper I knew, understood and loved little Sam Hamilton, boy preacher from Frostbite, Arkansas. Even though I had not fully developed his character, I met him in high school, struggled with him in college and seminary, wept with him in the early years of his ministry, and enjoyed the peace of God he found as his life moved toward its summation.

So this is not really my story, but in some ways I wish it were mine. I like this kid. The more I wrote about him, the more I liked his family. Sure, I enjoyed the mentoring of my own Rev. Earl Lee and preached my own five-minute first sermon, but from that point forward, our paths diverged. Sam's story came forth from the mix of people I met along the way.

To satisfy my publisher, I will put in the usual disclaimer:

This book is a work of fiction. Names, characters, places and incidents are products of the author's imagination or are used fictitiously. Any resemblance to actual events or locales or persons living or dead is entirely coincidental.

But the fact is, I knew this kid. In the fertile sands of my imagination, I knew him as well as I have known members of my own family. His life unfolded before me in the way a child may know the tooth fairy or talk to his secret friend.

The more I got to know Sam, the more we talked, and the more he lived in my imagination. Yes, I think that is it. I knew this kid and I liked the kid I came to know.

As you read his story, you will learn that Sam was a product of the South. That was our kinship because I, too, am from the South — an important distinction because of the preconceived notion so many people have about people who are from that strange and distant part of our world. We talk different. I was speaking at a conference in Boston in the spring of 2001. About 10 minutes into my presentation, a fellow raised his hand and said, "Ben, could you talk faster? We can't listen that slow."

Not only do we talk slow but we also use words that are not in the average American's vocabulary. Until my mama died at the age of 84, I still called her "Mama." No self-respecting Southerner would call his mama "Mother" — that would be too formal and would not show the respect a good Southern woman deserves. I am not ashamed to let you know I called my daddy "Daddy." When I went home for Christmas from college in Texas, I went home to see my mama and my daddy. Some of those folks I ran around with went home to New York to see their mothers and their fathers, but they did a lot of other strange things as well. I always wondered what happened to their mamas and their daddies.

So when Sam talks about his mama and his daddy, he is using the language of the times, the language of the South. I have placed Sam's story in the South of the '50s. Things were different back then. In my own case, I used poor English. It wasn't that we were not taught proper English. Mrs. Caldwell, the toughest English teacher in the history of the world, saw to that instruction. While some of my New England friends might inquire of you, "From whence did you come?" (which might just be grammatically correct albeit a little stiff), we Arkansas boys would just ask, "Where'd y'all good folks come from?" It didn't bother us to end the sentence with a preposition. Shoot, most of us didn't know what a preposition even looked like much less how to use it in a sentence. We just wanted to know where the folks came from, and so we asked them in our own particular fashion.

Sam is like that. It is a reflection *of* the time, not a reflection *on* the time. It was a simple life our little friend was born into and, unfortunately, it did not stay that way.

It has been my own life experience that people from the South get stereotyped. While I may begin by placing that stereotype on Sam, it is because I am writing about a time when the grammar police were not standing on the doorstep and most people had never heard of being politically correct. I am pleased to say that, today, a person coming from our fictional Frostbite School System would speak with the same grammatical consciousness as anyone else in this nation. But regarding the time of Sam's story, that just was not the fact. It is a fact that I thought "ain't" was an active verb until I was writing my Master's thesis. Daddy taught me that the best explanation point a man could use in a sentence was a good "hell" or "damn."

So when I write about that time, it is not meant to make fun of or point an educated finger at a somewhat uneducated time. That was just the way we were in those days. By the way, I still think those days may well have been the proverbial "good old days." And somehow I think Sam might agree.

Yes, we were from the South, but to my knowledge none of my ancestors ever owned a slave. Never married his or her first cousin, though I will admit to having a crush on a certain aunt during my formative years — but I hasten to add nothing ever came of it. As far as I know, none of our clan ever drove a hot rod in a NASCAR race. Except for one time in my own pilgrimage when I was in graduate school and about to starve to death, no one ever lived in a trailer with more than six tires under it.

My parents were Southern parents. And despite the stereotype of the *Beverly Hillbillies,* the worst whipping I ever got was once when I came home and told my mama about something one of the "little nigger boys did downtown." Within five minutes of that conversation, I knew that whatever people of color were to be called, in our house the word did not begin with an N. I was taught that if a person was older than yourself, you called them "Mr." or "Mrs." You said "Yes, Ma'am" and "No, Sir." The significant point in those tender years was age, not color.

In the South of those days, people did things like "sit up with the dead." I mean, if a member of your family died, they sent him off to the funeral home to be stuffed (or whatever they do there), then they brought him home and, for about four days and nights, the corpse would be in a coffin in the living room. Neighbors would come by and bring chicken and biscuits and grits. Then they would look at the dead person and say things like "Don't he look natural?" or "I tell you, Ol' Jim never looked better."

The men of the community would come by and sit up with the family all night while Ol' Jim was in the living room. Usually the family would go to bed because they were sleepy from eating all the good food that had been brought, but the neighbors still "stayed up with the dead" as it was called. That is just the way it was done in the South where I was raised. That is the way it was done in the South of Sam's day too.

As an author, I struggled to tell a story that would portray a time when life was simple and uncomplicated. I might use words that are not politically correct and should not have been even in 1953. But they were the words of the time, and I would not be true to Sam's story if I did not give you a proper picture of life back then.

Those were the days before one of my high school buddies got his head shot off in Vietnam. Those were the days before the riots in the streets of Chicago during a political convention. Those were the days before Nixon lied to us, and before Clinton made a mockery of the presidency. Those were the days before ...

Well, you get the point. I miss those days because life was simple then. The black family down the dirt road from our house didn't have a lot to eat, but when I was there playing with their children, I was invited to sit and eat what they had. And the same was true at my house when the willow tree in our front yard was first base for the Saturday softball game. We just all were expected to go in and have a cookie and a Coke. Mama would not have had it any other way.

I knew things had changed when Mama and Daddy agreed to keep the Hispanic missionary, who came to minister to the migrant workers during the fall harvest, in their home for four months. That was the first I had ever seen of racial animosity. Good people of the church tried to talk them out of letting Bro. Romaz live with them. When the good people couldn't change my parents' mind about the matter, they just chose to shun my parents instead. For two years, no one in the church would socialize with my parents or even speak to them. This was in a small town with only one grocery store and a post office ... yet the hatred of the time was upon us.

On the other hand, to my knowledge, no white person in my hometown had a white sheet on a hanger in his closet. But sometimes the inner blackness could break through and would not have been any less harmful had a sheet been worn. I was just out of high school when Dr. Martin Luther King, Jr., first came on the scene. Had he come to my little town, I have no doubt stones would have been thrown. And by then — saved, sanctified and set apart or not — I very well could have been one of those throwing the stones.

As I look back on it, I liked the person my mama tried to make me become. Sometimes I am embarrassed by the me I became. Now, I wish I had marched in Selma. Back then I thought "they got what they deserved." But don't get me wrong, a lot of Yankees felt the same way. Just face it, we were all pretty stupid people back then.

I am a product of that time, that place, and those friends and family members who loved me and tried to make me more than I wanted to be.

As I share Sam's journey with you, in many ways it has been my own journey. It will be the journey of countless boys who passed through that time and place. We, as Sam, passed through those early years and moved on because life always moves on. The clock is always running and the hands are always turning toward the midnight of our lives.

I really mean it when I say Sam's story is his own, but in a way I wish it could have been mine. Our heritage was the same, but how we dealt with it was greatly different. In many ways, I think the Sam you will come to know in these pages may have chosen the more interesting path.

One

I THINK IT WAS THE WILLOW TREE that first captured my attention and transported me to a place long forgotten. Thirty years of life in Chicago caused me to move to the dusty folds of my mind, the memories of those early years in Frostbite, Arkansas. It was the summer of 2001 and I finally returned to visit my childhood home. For 30-plus years, the path I would trod on this return trip to the small country village was long delayed. Life filled with getting all those degrees, raising a family, and trying to bump the people above me off the corporate ladder simply did not leave time for this walk through the past.

But on that summer day, I returned to Frostbite for the dedication of a simple wooden plaque that would memorialize my mama, who had served in a small-town church for some 80 years.

Seldom recognized in life, she was to be remembered in death as one who touched the lives of everyone who passed through the Frostbite Baptist Church during her years of service there.

The plaque simply read:

In memory of Martha Hamilton
Who served her Lord in this place
for 80 years
and while doing so
touched our Lives

My name is Sam Hamilton and I am Martha's baby boy. She was indeed a fine Christian woman and she touched my life too. This is not her story, it is mine. But I must admit, were it told in her eyes, the words would be much the same.

The church where we worshipped was built of yellow brick, long since faded. On the ceiling, just above the pulpit, is a water stain about the size of a funeral home fan. This is where water came through the roof every time it rained for at least the last 25 years, as far back as I can remember. To the right of the pulpit is the Sunday record board. By its account, last Sunday, 58 people were in Sunday school and the weekly offering was $248.98. Accurate records were important at the Frostbite Baptist Church.

Back in 1994, Mama became feeble with age so we moved her from her little green house at the corner of Main and Fourth Street in Frostbite, Arkansas, to be with our family in Chicago. She hated the snow but she loved her family, and we all worked hard to build a life together there. For six years she lived with us, and then one day she died. Nothing dramatic took place. She simply got tired and laid down for a rest, never got up.

We took her back to Frostbite to be buried in a plot by my daddy who passed on a few years before her. The service was fitting for her life and it seemed as though the entire town of 170 people came by to tell "Aunt Martha" good-bye. She touched their lives just as she touched mine.

On the Sunday six years before her passing, when she attended her last service at Frostbite Baptist Church, the Sunday record board indicated 52 people in Sunday school and an offering of $197.77. So according to last week's report, six more people went to Sunday school and $51.21 more money was given to the church. People in Frostbite probably felt that was pretty good progress! But truth is, not much changed over the years since Mama had been gone.

After Mama's funeral, Sarah and I did not waste any time leaving Frostbite to get back to our busy lives in Chicago. Mama had been our last connection to Arkansas and so we had no reason for return. The people at the Memorial Garden Cemetery in Blytheville took care of the grave and sent me an annual invoice for services rendered. Sarah and I chose to remember Mama through the pictures, both real and in our minds, of our happy times together. Therefore, we never returned to the place where Mama was given life and where she lay in her grave awaiting the "great gettin' up morning" that she so often talked about, for which she so often longed.

And now, some seven years after that time of extreme sadness, we responded to a call from the pastor of the Frostbite Baptist Church informing us of the plaque that would be dedicated in Mama's memory. We had not yet met Bro. Thompson, but he seemed like a nice enough man. He invited us to be a part of the memorial service. Sarah placed a call to our twins, Kim and Karen, one in Texas and the other in California, and together with their families we all returned to Frostbite for the occasion. The service was on Sunday morning in the same little church where my life was greatly influenced, not only by Mama, but also by so many others.

After the dedication service, dinner was brought in by the Woman's Missionary Union and country-fried chicken and homemade apple pie were served to all who wished for some. Mrs. Hatfield brought her squash casserole and everybody made over it just as they had when I was a kid. (Back then, she had been a young bride and this was the only thing she could cook. Now at 80, it still seemed to be her favorite recipe.) It was a wonderful time, that time at the table with so many old friends. It was a special day set apart to remember a special life.

I do not remember why I chose to leave the festivities, but I found myself walking down the little gravel road that led west out of town. The day was warm — summer days in Arkansas usually are — so I threw my coat over my shoulder, loosened my tie, and started walking. I crossed Morgan's Creek, where Bobby Rogers threw Buddy Sizemore off the bridge and dang near killed him. We were all in the second grade at the time.

I have no recollection how Morgan's Creek got its name. As kids, we built rafts and floated down its muddy waters. I remember it being as big as the Mississippi. I remember the trees growing from its banks as towering oaks reaching far into the sky.

It was in this muddy creek that we skinny-dipped after school. It was right under its bridge that Carl Ann Cook decided that if the boys could enjoy the creek with nothing more than a smile on their face then she ought to be able to join them. She did! My, what a day. I think I was 12 at the time.

The bridge over the creek always seemed high and foreboding. Mama always warned us to be careful crossing the bridge when we were walking to town. After years of absence, had you asked me to describe this bridge, I would have described a massive structure over turbulent waters. As I approached Morgan's Creek, today I was absolutely amazed.

Oh, the trees were still there. I even crawled down the bank to find the initials I carved on the tallest of them all — it must have been at least six feet high. And the mighty waters of Morgan's Creek were not really like the great Mississippi at all. Maybe 10 feet across, lazily flowing along in slow motion, this creek that seemed so massive to me as a child was really just a Mississippi Delta drainage ditch that carried the excess water from the cotton fields when it rained.

And the bridge. The massive structure of my memories was made of wooden planks nailed to wooden crossbeams that held up over the years far better than some of us who crossed it. No wonder Mama warned us about the bridge. There were no side rails, just heavy wooden planks about the width of a car. This architectural wonder of my childhood was all of 12 feet long.

So I once again crossed the bridge over Morgan's Creek. This time not so afraid of the waters below, but a bit terrified of the memories on the other side. You see, this was the bridge that crossed the creek that led to the road that would take me back to the house where I lived as a boy with my mama, daddy, and older brother, Danny. The house was almost two miles out of town. The last time I walked this road, my feet were bare and Chicago was more than a lifetime away. But as I walked, it seemed I was moving further and further back in time to a place that held more memories than I might ever have imagined.

The willow tree captured my attention. As it came into view, I could see it still stood in front of the little four-room house where I was conceived, born, and allowed to live until going off to college. The years were not kind to the house. Most of its windows were covered with tin and the front porch listed to the left. But the tree was grown now, not stunted by the weekly pruning that came at the close of each Sunday service during my days there. As I approached the tree, there was the sense of returning to an old friend. A once-mutual enemy was now a piece of the mosaic that made up my life.

The day was getting hotter, this summer afternoon when we renewed our acquaintance. So I placed my jacket on the ground in such a way as to provide some protection from the ants and other insects that tortured my youth. The trunk of the willow became my backrest. A slight breeze hummed through the leaves letting me know I was not totally alone. Looking through the low-hanging branches, I could see the boundaries of what had been my world back then.

Old man Osborn's cotton farm was across the road to the east of my position under the tree. Looking north, I could see the remains of the old black church that had not been in use for 20 years or so. It was about to fall down and it seemed no one really cared. If I looked toward the south, I saw the gravel road that led to the highway to Memphis. And directly behind me to the west was the house. I was surrounded by the compass points of memories.

Across old man Osborn's field, I could see the water tower in Frostbite, Arkansas. It too was faded and only the faint outline of the once-proud announcement that this was the "Home of the Frostbite Blizzards" remained. I played on the junior varsity team. We were the Breezes. Our name never made the water tower.

Today was Sunday. The cotton compress was shut down in honor of the Lord's Day, but on any other day I could have seen the smoke from the press. I once sat under this tree and counted 45 bales of cotton pressed in one hour just by watching the smoke rise like a signal from a Chickasaw village that might have once been located exactly on this spot. Mama worked at the press and verified my count later that evening. I was pretty proud of myself for getting it right. Then Mama wanted to know what I was doing wasting my time counting smoke puffs from the compress. Guess we took different views on things because at the time it seemed pretty important to me.

Overhead a hawk circled, riding the currents of the warm summer air. When we lived in this house, a hawk once killed one of our chickens and my daddy tried to shoot it out of the air. Might have worked had the hawk not taken a quick dive and had my daddy not followed the hawk to the ground before shooting. Killed one of our dogs, I can't remember which one, but the hawk got away. Daddy said we had too many dogs anyway. Just wondering today if that might be that same old hawk. I hear some of them live up to 50 years. Maybe it is, maybe it isn't. Who knows?

If I strained real hard and shaded my eyes, I could see the church from here. Long after the original building was built, on top of the church steeple they added a cross. Even sitting under the willow today, I could see just the tip of that cross. The water tower, puffs of smoke from the compress, and a slight glimpse of the church. Even a circling hawk. It was good to be back home. I never thought I would say that, but it was true.

From Frostbite to Chicago. From trying to make out with some preadolescent classmate in the backseat of a '54 Impala to a wife and two great children. It had been one hell of a journey.

Two

So much of my life was connected to the little church where, not an hour before, I sat talking and laughing with long-forgotten friends. Mama's life had pretty much been the focus of the entire service this morning. Maybe that is why, at the end, Bro. Thompson called on me to say the Benediction. That was sort of nice because as far back as I can remember going to church, the Benediction seemed to be the very best part of the service. There was always such majesty in how the service was closed. Being good Baptists, we always closed the service with the invitation hymn during which sinners were saved, backsliders were forgiven and, when it was over, you got to go home.

Bro. Earl Lee was the pastor of Frostbite Baptist Church during all the years before I left home to go to college. In our little church in Frostbite, Arkansas, no one could close out a service like Bro. Earl Lee. First, Bro. Earl Lee could preach for an hour and a half, always screaming at the top of his voice, before coming to that closing part. As he began to slow down — as the sweat ran from his forehead like a river — old Bro. Earl Lee would tell everyone to stand and sing that great gospel hymn "Just As I Am."

Now on a good day, we might have had 50 people in the service. If it rained or if the St. Louis Cardinals had an early game, we topped out at around 25. But regardless of the number of people present, old Bro. Earl Lee laid into that invitation full force because in his mind he was jerking people from the "mouth of hell itself!" And you would always have to sing until *someone* made a *decision.* I remember one time when, after singing about 10 verses with no visible results, I decided to go forward. I was maybe 10 years old at the time and had not accumulated enough sin to really fit the category of backslider, but it was obvious if no one went forward we were going to be there all day.

So there I was at the front of the church with Bro. Earl Lee. I never will forget his voice in my ear as he whispered, "Now, boy, why are you down here at the front right now?"

I whispered back in his ear, "'Cause if don't nobody else come forward, Bro. Earl Lee, we gonna be here all day."

Suddenly, he started groaning in the Spirit. It went something like this: "Thank you, Jesus. Thank you, Lord. Bless this child who has come to You today to confess his sins. Bless Jesus. Thank you, Lord." Etc., etc.

This went on for about five minutes until most of the people figured I was a mass murderer or something. Lord knows I didn't know what was going on. I was just trying to get the service over, but if Bro. Earl Lee needed to use me for an example of God's saving power, I was ready to be used. *Just get this thing over and let's go home!* Finally the groaning stopped, someone said a prayer, and we went home.

On the way home, my mama, who I will admit was as godly a woman as has ever walked this earth, said to me, "What did you tell the preacher this morning?"

"I just told him I was coming up front so he could close the service." It was the truth, nothing I need fear.

"You didn't confess no sins or nothing?" Mama asked.

"No, Mama."

"Well, you know what that means. When we get home, get me a switch off that willow tree and let's really close the service."

So the Sunday ritual continued. Every Sunday the service would close and for some reason, usually greatly deserved, I would get a whipping with a switch cut from the weeping willow tree in our front yard. Every Sunday I had either been too loud or had not participated enough. I had not been on time or I had stayed too late. Lord knows, I just never could seem to get it right. When I left for college, that tree still had not grown taller than my head. In fact, it was not until I went to the seminary that I found out that the whipping at the end of the service was not a part of the ritual!

• • •

I like the way different denominations close their services. You take the Methodists, for instance. They have that invitation stuff too, but they don't waste any time about it. You have one verse to get from hell into heaven. If you don't make the trip, then you better hope you live till next week and get another chance to get right with the Lord.

The Presbyterians have it down. They usually put a card in the pew that says something like "If you want to go to heaven, give us your name and address and we will call you." Let's don't waste any time trying to get you down the aisle. Just sign the card and we will write your name in the Book, but for right now the ball game is almost on the radio, so let's get out of here and find out if the St. Louis Cardinals are winning.

The Episcopalians are really good. They close with Holy Communion, then everyone stands still while the top priest and a lot of other people dressed in white carry the cross down the aisle and out the door. If you are a Baptist, it is like the closing of Vacation Bible School.

But if you really want to get home, you need to become a Catholic. I'm telling you they just amaze me. The minute they get Holy Communion, they are out the door. The priest may still be talking, but the people are already at Denny's ordering the chili burger. At least that is what I have been told. We didn't have any Catholic folks in Frostbite, Arkansas. Around here it was thought that if you weren't a Methodist or a Baptist, then probably some Yankee had been messing with you.

Anyway, those of us of the Baptist persuasion never made it to the restaurant or, as in my case, home for Sunday dinner before about 1 o'clock. When you had Bro. Earl Lee yanking people from the Gates of Hell, it just took longer than one verse and a prayer.

•••

I was a long way from my life in Chicago. In Chicago, Sarah and I had become members of a church. But it was a church far removed from the church that engulfed me with memories on this hot summer day under an old willow tree on a dusty road in northeast Arkansas.

Funny how the mind works. I had not thought on such things for years, but sitting under this old tree I was reminded of some of the lessons Bro. Earl Lee once shouted at the top of his voice to all who would listen.

Standing as tall as a Chicago Bull's center, he would preach at the top of his lungs:

THE SPIRITUAL WALK MUST BEGIN SOMEWHERES. BLESS GOD, IT DON'T JUST HAPPEN. PRAISE GOD, YOU AIN'T BORNED INTO IT. You ain't going to inherit it from your parents. Walking with Jesus starts when you make up your mind to accept the fact that, as a blasted sinner, someone has to pay for your sin. Bless Jesus. They have to go down to the jailhouse and bail you out of jail, so to speak. Praise God, that is what the Lord Jesus did for us on the Cross. He said, "Boys, you have sinned, but I ain't gonna take it out on you. I'm looking to pay the price for you. I will give My life in order for you to be forgiven." BLESS GOD! AND THANK YOU, JESUS!

Oh, man, could that old preacher preach. There might not be 20 of us in the congregation and everyone there could be a saint in the eyes of God, but Bro. Earl Lee preached every Sunday on Jesus and hell. His catchphrase was "I'll yank them out of hell and let someone else teach them how to live." In my youth, I saw Bro. Earl Lee do a lot of yanking.

He preached hard on the eternal fact that Jesus paid the price of sin for us and it just stands to reason that we must accept it. That old man would rave and rant up and down the aisle of the church just scaring the hell out of most of us. He made a big deal out of the fact that he wanted every "Godless soul on this Godforsaken earth to make a personal decision about Jesus." And the way he said it, "Jesus" was drug out to become a four-syllable word! I will have to admit that old preacher had the emphasis on the right point as far as he was concerned. There would come a time when I had a little trouble with it all, but that was a few years down the road. Right now, there seemed to be some comfort in the memories.

•••

When I was about 13 years old, I used to go with Bro. Earl Lee down to the County Penal Farm to preach to the "poor lost souls locked up in jail" as he liked to call them. You have not really seen a real hell-fire and brimstone preacher in action until you have gone to the County Jail where he has a captive audience. I must have gone with him 10 or 15 times over the years. Every time, he used the same illustration to those prisoners. Never in all my time of going with him did he ever change it. And every time he told it, he would get real quiet like he was telling them something that was a real secret. Shoot, some of the lifers could probably tell it better than Bro. Earl Lee could.

I used to get a kick at how dramatic he would make it. Bro. Earl Lee would be preaching along, shouting to the High Heavens and then, all of a sudden, he would almost shut down to a whisper to set the stage:

Let's just assume for a moment that you are down there in Cummins's Prison and you are about an hour from being executed. Old Smokey is just waiting for your old sinful ass.

And just as they take you into the death chamber, the warden calls the governor and says, "Governor, I really like this guy. I know he has committed a terrible crime, but he has potential. So if you don't mind, I would like to be executed in his place."

Then the governor says, "Put that mean SOB on the phone."

To the poor lost soul, "Boy, did you hear what the warden just said?"

"Yes, sir, I did" that lost soul would reply.

And Bro. Earl Lee would put the facts in focus:

The governor, he's fired up at you now, "Boy, you listen to me, you sorry devil. I am going to go along with it. Whether you want him to or not, I am going to let the warden be fried in your place.

"Now here is the deal. He is going to die for you. When that happens, you have one of two choices. You can go back to your cell and stay in prison for the rest of your sorry life, or you can accept the fact that the warden died for you and you are free to go home and start life over with a clean slate. Now what do you want to do?"

Things would be real quiet, then Bro. Earl Lee would continue:

You think about it a moment and you decide that going home sounds A Whole Lot Better! than living the rest of your life in that 6-by-8 cell so you say, "Governor, I'm thinking I will just accept what the warden just done for me, and I'm thinking I will go home."

Then Bro. Earl Lee would look those prisoners in the face and shout at the top of his voice:

BLESS GOD! THAT'S WHAT JESUS DONE FOR YOU. Now take it or leave it, but that's the deal.

We would sing a song and one by one some of those hardened prisoners would come forward to give their lives to Jesus. Bro. Earl Lee had come through again.

• • •

Bro. Earl Lee's way of closing the service was about as good a closing act as we ever saw around Frostbite,

Arkansas. It made no difference to Bro. Earl Lee where he was. He could be preaching at his church, under a tent, in front of a jail cell or behind the house, but he always closed the service for Jesus, as he would say, by trying to get "poor sinners to come forward and give they heart to Jesus!"

He always said that the closing of the service provided those of us who attended the Frostbite Baptist Church an opportunity to tell or show others that we had accepted what God had done for us, that we had used our "get out of jail free card."

The closing of the service was not a casual ritual with Bro Earl Lee. He really believed it was very often the deciding moment in a person's life. Hearing him preach one made it pretty easy to believe that too.

The best thing about Bro. Earl Lee was that he could adapt that closing to just about any situation. One day I was standing in our yard looking out across the road to where Torn Hawkins was driving a tractor for Mr. Osborn. Mama had sent me out with a nice cool drink for Torn. She was always doing something saintly like that, and I was usually the messenger. I guess I was around 12 years old at the time. Torn stopped his tractor under the pecan tree that stood in the middle of the field and took the water from me. We were just standing there in the shade of that tree when Bro. Earl Lee drove up.

He had been working on Torn's eternal salvation for some time and Torn was no closer to heaven than he had ever been. This time Bro. Earl Lee started in on Torn about coming to church. Torn explained the necessity of plowing the field on Sunday because it had been raining a lot and he had to plow every time he could. Then Torn made the mistake of saying, "But Earl Lee, the next time you get me in church, I am going to give my life to Jesus."

Well, that was all Bro. Earl Lee had been waiting for. Suddenly he had Torn right where he wanted and he lit in on the man right there.

"Torn, you sorry, no-good sinner. Don't you know you don't have to come to church to accept the Lord Jesus?

"In the Bible, old Saul of Tarsus made his decision while taking a trip across country to kill Christians. They is a bunch of stories about people sitting at home, working or driving in they car when they just suddenly decided to do it.

"Good Lord, Torn, you never told me you was waiting to come to church to get saved. Get on your knees, boy, 'cause we gonna get you saved right here and now."

Before Torn knew what hit him, Bro. Earl Lee had him on his knees and praying, "Father, I accept the fact that I am a sinner and that Jesus died for my sins. Please forgive me of those sins and let Jesus come into my life and live through me. Amen."

To my knowledge, and I could be wrong, but I do believe that from the next Sunday until I went to college some six years later I don't think Torn Hawkins ever missed a Sunday in church. Forced into the Kingdom by a mad-man preacher may have been the procedure, but the cure seemed to take.

•••

Another time when I went with Bro. Earl Lee to the County Penal Farm, he and I got to talking about this saving stuff and had what was probably the only serious talk we ever truly engaged in.

I remember he said to me, "Sam, it is the simplicity that complicates it. We go to a Baptist service and hear some country preacher, or we go to an Episcopal service and see the ritual, and sometimes we get confused. When in reality all it takes is one sinner, approaching the one God, and asking for forgiveness and receiving it.

"Any way you look at it, that's not a bad deal."

He didn't call me "boy." He wasn't yelling or screaming about something. At that very moment with this country preacher, I connected. Maybe I could learn something from him after all.

• • •

Suddenly my watch beeped the hour and brought me out of my reverie. It was almost 3 o'clock and, by now, the dinner at the church would be about over. I knew Sarah enough to know that she would be the last one there, cleaning up the mess made by a bunch of hungry Baptists.

I dialed her cell phone number. Signals flashed across the sky and around the country and in a second her phone rang not two miles from where I was sitting. "Hi, Luv. Just checking in."

She sounded a little bit concerned, "Sam, where are you? Someone said they saw you leave about an hour ago. Where are you?"

"I'm out at the old home-place. Think you and the kids can kill an afternoon somewhere?"

Ever supportive, she said, "Sure, what's up?"

"Oh, not much. I would just sort of like the afternoon out here by myself for a while. Got a little thinking to do. Could you come back and pick me up at the church around six?"

As always, she understood. No more questions, no more explanations were needed. Just "I love you, Sam. See you around six."

I had a lot of remembering to do as I sat under this old tree on this lazy summer day. I could not help but chuckle at how many times I had prayed that Mama would forget the unofficial close to the service and just let me have lunch. She never did forget and, if truth be known, I probably never did deserve to have her forget so at the end of the day the score was about even.

Three

SECOND TO ACCEPTING JESUS as your Lord and Savior, the next big step, according to Bro. Earl Lee, was to "get your prayer engine going." Lord only knows what he meant by that, but between his preaching on Sunday both morning and night and the regular Wednesday evening prayer service, we at the Frostbite Baptist Church were convinced that prayer was pretty important. There was a big sign up at the front of the church: *Prayer is a wonderful thing!* The words were printed on cardboard, then framed.

Prayer may be a wonderful thing, but for me it just didn't always work. I spent many a ride home from church praying that the willow tree would be dead with all its limbs fallen to the ground. Never happened.

And sometimes when prayer did work, the end results were not what I had expected. I once spent one whole summer praying for a date with Sue Ann Middleton and, when I finally got it, the night was spent with Sue Ann and her daddy watching "The Texaco Hour with Milton Berle" on TV. That was about the most boring date I had experienced up to the young age that I was at that time. (There would be many others that followed.) But that one night with Sue Ann and her daddy taught me early on to be careful what you pray for because you might just get it.

My friend Gary Lynn Houston had a theory about prayer that I think had some potential merit. Gary Lynn was about three years younger than I was, but I dated his sister Shirley for a while and from then on he stuck pretty close to me. I liked him. He was like the kid brother I never had. Most of all, he had lots of crazy theories about religion and stuff.

For instance, his theory was you prayed for something, and then whatever it took to answer that prayer was "God's will." Now you take the fact that we were raised in northeast Arkansas where the summers are hotter than hell and there is nothing better than a watermelon eaten in the middle of a cotton field, and you will begin to get the picture.

One day Gary Lynn and I were sitting around talking about things and we drifted off on the subject of prayer. In northeast Arkansas, a lot of things were centered around religion — mainly because to get religion was about as good as anything that was gonna happen to you around there. Anyway, Gary Lynn suggested his theory about God answering prayer. The dialogue went like this:

"Ham, you want a watermelon?" Gary Lynn always shortened my name and called me Ham. I didn't like it, but it caught on and I was pretty much stuck with it.

"Yea, but ours ain't ripe yet."

"You seen them melons over at Miss Johnson's field?"

"Yea, they been eaten them for a week."

"Well, let's pray for one of them melons," he suggested.

"What good's that gonna do us if they belong to Miss Johnson? She ain't gonna give us one."

"I don't know, but the preacher said God answers prayer so let's try it," he offers.

Well, my pious friend got down on his knees and confessed his sins, most of which I didn't know about and if my mama had known about I would not have been out there with him anyway. He promised to do better. He praised the Lord and then he made his pitch:

Lord, You know it is hot and we need a watermelon. And Lord, You know the best watermelons in this county are not one-half mile from here in Miss Johnson's patch. So Lord, we ask You now to show us a way to get one of them melons. And Lord, when You do, we will do everything in our power to fulfill Your will.

Then Gary Lynn got up off his knees, dusted his jeans, and sat back against the barn.

"You think the Lord's gonna answer that prayer?" I asked.

"I think He will show us how, yes, I do."

"You really do all that stuff you confessed?"

"Well some of it I made up 'cause the Lord likes to hear all that bad stuff so He can forgive."

"Well, we still ain't got no melon," I said in my heathen unbelief.

"It's coming to me," he whispered. "Yes, sir, it is coming to me. The Lord just told me that Miss Johnson is gone from home and if we go right now, we can get one of the melons from her watermelon patch and no one will ever know."

"Sounds a whole lot like stealing to me," I was still in need of convincing.

"Nah, it's the Lord's will so let's get going."

Sure enough Miss Johnson was not home. We carried out the Lord's will by getting ourselves a good 15-pounder then sitting behind the barn for about an hour in the shade eating it.

I guess it was okay because Gary Lynn went on to be a Sunday school teacher in a big church over in Jonesboro.

•••

Bro. Earl Lee used to preach a lot about prayer. He believed in laying on of hands and praying for people. Most folks around our parts said he was pretty good at it.

I can only remember one case where it seemed like his prayers were not taking effect and it took a lot of laying on of hands.

Flo Ellen England was a fine young lady "in the maturing stage" as my daddy used to say. She was a big-chested girl from about 13 years of age on. Well, I remember in high school she came down with the bronchitis or something like that, and Bro. Earl Lee went over to her house and laid hands on her chestal regions. It must have been a terrible sickness she had because Bro. Earl Lee kept going over and praying and laying his hands on Flo Ellen's chest until her daddy threatened to shoot him if he ever came back.

I don't know what the fuss was all about because Flo Ellen was pretty open to that laying on of hands with or without prayer. In fact, we used to have mini healing services with her out in the parking lot of the Kream Kastle most Saturday nights.

Anyway, after that experience, the deacons met and told Bro. Earl Lee to go easy on the laying on of hands and place a little more faith in prayer. I guess it worked because when I left home he was still preaching and praying and, from time to time, laying on a hand or two. Flo Ellen got healed and, as far as I know, never had the disease of the chestal regions again.

•••

Thinking back to before I was even out of grade school, seems I was always interested in how people talked to God. Some could just get to the point while others had to bring God up to date on everything before getting down to the petition stuff.

I remember Mr. Forsyth, a deacon of good standing in our church, used to begin every prayer with, "Lord, as you read in the *Memphis Commercial Appeal* this week" — I was never sure why God had to read things in the newspaper, but for whatever reason Mr. Forsyth thought it important to remind God where he got his information.

My daddy was big on short prayers. We always liked it when he asked the Lord's blessings on the food. He would bow his head and fold his hands and pray, "Good Lord, good meat. Thank you, Lord. Now let's eat." And we would dig in. Can't beat a good, short prayer.

I think for most of us kids, our most often-said prayer was, "Dear Lord, don't let the preacher call on Mr. B.J. Forsyth to pray." That prayer was never answered in all of my growing-up years. No matter how late the service had gone. No matter how hungry all of us were. Bro. Earl Lee just would have to call on Mr. Forsyth to say the Benediction.

Now Mr. Forsyth was a fine deacon in the church and a good neighbor to my grandma, but you gave him an audience and he would pray till the sun went down.

He always prayed for the "boys overseas who are fighting to keep the Communist devils from our shore." Now I never was much on history, but this would have been about 1949. As far as I know WWII was over, Korea had not started, and we didn't *have* any boys fighting overseas. But Mr. Forsyth prayed for them anyway. Mama had a brother who was a pilot in WWII, flew the Hump some 23 times during those years. Mama always thought it was Mr. Forsyth's prayers that kept her brother safe. Maybe so, but six weeks after her brother came back home he got in a fight at the Veteran's Hall in Osceola and got shot dead. Guess Mr. Forsyth stopped praying for him a little too soon.

Anyway, once Mr. Forsyth got called on to pray in church and after the international affairs were taken care of with the Lord, he would move to Step 2. That was when he would start with Bro. Earl Lee and go around the room and pray for everyone in the church service by name. And just to let us know that he knew what was going on around town, he would usually confess our sins for us too.

Now Lord, You know that Hamilton boy and Gary Lynn Houston stole a watermelon from Miss Johnson's field this week and I pray You forgive them of the sin of stealing.

About that time I would be seeing the willow tree and losing my total train of thought on Mr. Forsyth's prayer. That old man was really good at confessing just enough sin on everyone there to keep the town all stirred up for the next week.

Lord, forgive R.C. for You-Know-What-He-Is-Doing and I pray You bring him back into the fold.

Mr. R.C. owned the local grocery store. Mr. Forsyth may have known what R.C. was doing, but the rest of us didn't have a clue. R.C.'s wife sure didn't know, but finding out became her primary job for the next week or two. Down at the post office on Monday, neighbors would be wondering about R.C. Yes, R.C. would be the talk of the town all just because Mr. Forsyth had confessed R.C.'s sin right in the middle of the closing prayer.

Of course, it was not uncommon the next time Mr. Forsyth was called on to pray for him to clarify:

And Lord, I was mistaken about R.C. when we talked a few weeks ago. I thank You for his upstanding place in this community.

In the meantime, R.C.'s wife had not spoken to him in three weeks, little kids were not allowed to go into his store, and he was thinking about hitching the next train to Chicago.

But old Bro. Forsyth did clear up the situation with the Lord.

Yes sir, prayer is a funny thing. And at the Frostbite Baptist Church, whether there were 20 people present or 50, at the close of the service you could hear them all praying in unison under their breath, "Lord, please don't let Bro. Earl Lee call on Mr. B.J. Forsyth to pray."

•••

Most of the kids in Frostbite, Arkansas, had a little trouble with the whole idea of prayer. We wondered why prayer mattered if God already made up His mind about how things were going to work out. That used to bother me a lot too. About the only one who seemed to make any sense on the subject was Bro. Webb down at the Methodist church.

One night after Methodist Youth Fellowship (MYF), a group of us kids were talking with Bro. Webb about this prayer stuff. He read us Jonah 3:10. God told Jonah to go to Nineveh and tell all the bad people there that He was going to destroy them because they were such a mean lot.

But a strange thing happened. The people heard Jonah and they started praying for forgiveness, promised to do better ... and all that stuff. The Bible says:

And God saw their works, that they turned from their evil way; and God repented of the evil, that he had said that he would do unto them; and he did it not.
Jonah 3:10 KJV

Leroy Evers, who was about as holy as any high school kid could have been, jumped up and clapped his hands and started walking around the room. He said, "My Lord, Bro. Webb, that's heavy stuff any way you look at it. Do you mean to tell me that God was all prepared to wipe them out, but they prayed and God *changed His mind?* Sweet Jesus, just think about it. Looks to me like there are all kinds of things we can change if we just get around to asking the good Lord to change them."

Bro. Webb allowed that to be about right and things began to settle down again. From my perspective as a

Baptist boy in a Methodist meeting, I decided I had better keep my mouth shut. But right there I was getting the point — ain't no doubt about that. Seemed to me that prayer was about the best thing we had going. I figured there was a whole lot of things I might begin praying on as soon as I got out of that meeting.

On the walk home afterwards, I got to thinking. In our church, Bro. Earl Lee had built what he called a prayer chain. Let's say you had a family problem and wanted to pray to God and ask Him to solve your problem. You could do that all by yourself, or you could call my mama, who was the Prayer Captain. Then she would call two people, and they would call three people, and in about 10 minutes, the whole town would be praying for you.

Fortunately, you didn't have to tell Mama what the problem was. You just let her know there was a need in your life and she would get the ball rolling. Of course by the second level, everybody in town was speculating on what the problem was and, by the second day, you had folks praying for all sorts of problems in your life. I guess the best you could hope for was that one of them would hit the right thing and God would do some answering for you.

I figured that was what Bro. Webb was trying to teach us because that is exactly what happened in Nineveh. A group of people prayed, asked God to do something, and God changed His mind.

The more I walked and thought, the more it seemed that was the dicey part. *What if God does not always do what we want Him to do? What if He sees the big picture and, since we are His children, He looks out for our best interests?*

Bro. Earl Lee used to tell us about his brother from up in Missouri. To hear Bro. Earl Lee tell it, his brother decided the Lord wanted him to go over to Paragould and do a little squirrel hunting with some of his friends. To put a little pressure on his dad, the boy mentioned that he had prayed to be able to go. His daddy thought about it for a time and just decided it wasn't the thing his son needed to do.

Well, Bro. Earl Lee's brother was totally disillusioned with prayer. In fact, he told his daddy that there was nothing to this prayer stuff because he had really prayed to go and God didn't come through. Like daddies do sometimes, his daddy didn't fall for that line either and still didn't let him go.

A week later, on the way home from hunting, his friends were in a car wreck. The boy's best friend was killed, and the other two passengers were seriously hurt. Bro. Earl Lee used to ask us, "Did God answer his prayer or did God look at the big picture and do what was best for my brother?" That was one to make you stop and think.

I never did know whether that was a true story or not. Bro. Earl Lee never did tell us his brother's name. Another thing we all knew was that sometimes Bro. Earl Lee would make up a story just to make a point. I don't think that is lying in the real sense, but Bro. Earl Lee seemed to do it about every Sunday.

I tell you one thing, after he told us that story about his brother (real or made up), we started looking at prayer in a whole lot different way. We decided it wasn't about *What's in it for me?* so much as *What does the big picture look like?*

Bro. Earl Lee wasn't one to encourage spiritual thinking a lot, but he got us on this one. Gary Lynn Houston and I didn't do a lot of watermelon stealing after that experience. The big picture seemed to point out that the good Lord might just *change His mind* on our needing one of them melons and let Miss Johnson blow our damn heads off.

•••

On another night, a bunch of us kids were down at the Methodist church playing on their pool table. I'm here to tell you, the Methodist kids had it a whole lot better than us Baptists. They could shoot pool and dance and, to my knowledge, there was no danger of getting pregnant by doing either activity.

But while we were over there, Bro. Webb came in and we got to talking about this prayer stuff again. He said that prayer is also at times a petition to God to share with Him my desires. Let's say your wife has cancer so you pray for her to be healed. Sometimes God answers that prayer just as you want it answered and sometimes He looks at the big picture and doesn't heal her. Confusing? Sometimes it is. But Bro. Webb said, "Prayer ain't so much the way for us to change God's mind, but it is a way God changes us to accept His will."

Another thing Bro. Webb taught us was when we pray the words are *unimportant.* I used to think you had to talk in King James Bible English, but that is not true. Bro. Webb said we ought to talk to God as we would talk to a friend. Not to be sacrilegious, but it might go something like this if God's name was Bob:

Bob, I have a problem. All of my life I have been abusing our friendship. I have lied, stolen, and done a thousand things to hurt you. I am so ashamed. Will you forgive me? If you will, I promise that with your help from this day on I will be the best friend you have ever had. And if I do slip back into my old ways, I promise to come to you and tell you about it and ask you to forgive me again.

Those were formative days in my prayer life. Just seemed to me like, all in all, it was pretty simple. It is one person talking to another person (God) as one talks to a friend. I guess the big thing I learned during that time was that Mr. Forsyth had it all wrong.

As much as I would hate to tell him and mess up all his long and involved confessing of the communities' collective sin, the fact is that only I can confess my sin.

I may have been a kid, but I was learning.

Four

AFTER I GREW UP AND GOT OUT in the world and studied some of the great religions of the world, I came to understand that there are just some things required by every religion. If you are going to be counted among that flock, there are just some things you better accept or get out.

But growing up in Frostbite, Arkansas, we were not overly sophisticated in world religions. In fact, we had four churches.

There was the First Methodist Church on Main Street where Bro. Webb was pastor. Bro. Webb was bigger than a house and once got stuck in Jerry Stillman's new MG automobile. They had to call a mechanic from Blytheville to take the steering wheel off to get Bro. Webb out or he might have preached that Sunday in the parking lot.

There was the Christ of Christ (long before any of that "united" stuff was added). There was the First Baptist Church, which was the black Baptist church located behind Mr. R.C's store. And there was the Frostbite Baptist Church, which was the white Baptist church located on Main Street just down from First Methodist.

It happened well before my time, but as the story is told, there was almost a riot in town when the black folks started the first Baptist church in Frostbite and proceeded, without permission some might add, to take the name of First Baptist Church. No self-respecting white person was going to go to a "Second" Baptist Church if the First Baptist Church was a black congregation. *Lord forbid that they should all just worship together.* So after a two-hour business meeting, the white church decided to just be the Frostbite Baptist Church and be second to no one.

Back in those days, the good people of the white Baptist church would sing, "Red and yellow, black and white, they are precious in His sight. Jesus loves the little children of the world." The good people would sing that, but it meant that He loved *them* as long as *they* stayed in *their place* and didn't come to the Frostbite Baptist Church.

•••

Every church in Frostbite, Arkansas, had its own requirements. And just like the great world religions, if you were going to be counted among the flock, you had to adhere to those requirements.

Now you take the Methodist church for instance. In Frostbite, the Methodists were the "uppity" group, as my mama would describe them. We didn't have any Episcopalians so being Methodist was as uppity as you could get in Frostbite.

The Methodist church was brick. Not just any brick, it was constructed of antique red brick. When it was built, my daddy took one look at it and said, "If they was gonna spend all that money to build the damn thing, why did they build it to look so old?"

Mama told him he was going to hell for using the D word, but she also wondered aloud why they built it to look so old. Frankly, I was only about 13 years old then and I didn't really care if it looked old. The only thing I cared about was the fact that the Methodists had all the rich kids going there and they were allowed to *dance.* They even danced at MYF, which was held right there in the church every Sunday night.

Over at the Baptist church, we were taught that dancing led to some terrible sinning and when carried too far could actually lead to having a baby. To show how this worked, Bro. Earl Lee usually got us boys off to the side and told us about Pepper Johnson's wife, Betty Lou. Betty Lou and Pepper were high school sweethearts and went to every dance in the county. Before you knew it, Betty Lou had four kids and still had not gotten Pepper down the aisle. For the most part, us Baptist kids stayed away from that dancing stuff.

So it is pretty reasonable for a big part of the town to believe that dancing on Sunday night at MYF was pretty serious stuff. In fact, as I figured it, at that one event they did enough sinning to bust hell wide open. First, *they danced,* which any self-respecting Baptist will tell you leads to other things too terrible to mention in mixed company. Second, they were dancing *in the church.* Never mind that in the Old Testament they were always dancing around the Temple, in Frostbite, Arkansas, it was a mortal sin to dance in the church as far as my tribe was concerned. And then third — to top it all off — they danced, in the church, *on Sunday.*

Bless his heart, if not another sin was ever committed within 90 miles of Frostbite, just the stuff going on down at the Methodist church was enough to keep Bro. Earl Lee going till the Lord called him home.

This was especially fun every year when the senior prom came around. A dance would always be planned and the Methodist women would go all out planning it. Over at our Baptist church, Bro. Earl Lee was raising Cain about the sinful dancing and saying that any of us Baptist kids who went to that hellhole would be doomed forever. That will really get in your mind when you are trying to decide who to take to the prom. I mean, a one-time date at the senior prom was one thing, but spending an eternity in hell with that same girl was worth giving some thought to.

But anyway, as I figured it out, there were three things you had to do to be a Methodist. First, you had to be *baptized as a baby.* Now that was fine with me, but a lot of folks got real upset about it. I used to listen hour after hour as my folks talked about the baby baptizing going on down at the Methodist church. It was several years later that I learned they were not really baptizing babies at all. At most, they were just sprinkling a little water on the kids' heads so I couldn't figure out what all the fuss was about.

Second, you had to *dress nice* when you went to church. St. Patrick's Day in New York City didn't have one thing on the First Methodist Church of Frostbite, Arkansas, when it came to the women of the church dressing up for Easter. I remember one time when Rose Ann Hill went to church — the Methodist one, because Rose Ann was about as uppity as you could get. She was dressed in a black dress with big white polka dots on it. And to top it off, so to speak, she had a black hat with big white polka dots to match.

Just as we were riding up in our pick-up to go to the Frostbite Baptist Church for the Easter service, good ol' Rose Ann came prancing down the street. There was a lot of discussion among us with the consensus being that she better stay away from the barn because she looked a whole lot like a Guernsey heifer. You ain't gonna believe this but, from that day forth, my saintly, Baptist mama called her "that Methodist heifer." I thought that was rather tacky myself. I thought Rose Ann was just being a good Methodist.

And finally, to be a good Methodist, you had to have a service that was short enough to *beat the Baptists to the restaurant for Sunday dinner.* In that regard, Bro. Webb was the man for the Methodist church. That man could get it over in a flash and get to Miss Hawkins' BBQ restaurant before Bro. Earl Lee had even warmed up real good.

In the Methodist denomination, you don't get to pick your own pastor. The Bishop does that for you. It's a good thing too because the Methodists in Frostbite would never have gotten anyone if it had been a private choice. But the Bishop sent Bro. Webb, then a young man of 27, to be pastor of the First Methodist Church of Frostbite, Arkansas. At that time I am told he weighed about 145 pounds and looked real good in his double-breasted suit.

I am also told he had great ambitions to go on to a larger congregation, which would not have taken much to accomplish. Any church that had more than 30 members would have been a step up for Bro. Webb. But bless his heart, he made the mistake of getting in the habit of preaching seven-minute sermons. That started a chain reaction of great love and affection for him by those who went to his church. So every time the Bishop thought about moving Bro. Webb, Mr. Ledbetter, who was the richest man in the county, wrote to the Bishop and told him that if he moved Bro. Webb, he would never see another dime of Mr. Ledbetter's hard-earned money. Even the Bishop knew the odds of getting any big money out of old Ledbetter were pretty slim, but there were just some chances he didn't want to take, and messing with Mr. Ledbetter was one such chance.

So by the time I came into my early teen years and started having ambitions of my own, Bro. Webb had been in Frostbite for 22 years, weighed 432 pounds, and wore a size 62 custom-made blue suit with a hole in the back pocket.

But anyway, that's why the Methodists beat the Baptists to the restaurants on Sunday and why being willing to get out early was one of the prerequisites of being a Methodist in Frostbite, Arkansas. Over at the Frostbite Baptist Church, we didn't think we had been to church unless Bro. Earl Lee preached for an hour and a half. Sometimes at the First Baptist Church, they praised the Lord all day and into the night.

• • •

The Church of Christ was diagonally across from my grandmother's house. It was a little, white-framed building. The yard around the church was always trimmed very nicely, but no one — and I mean no one from the Methodist or the Baptist groups, to my knowledge — had ever set foot inside the Church of Christ building. I grew up thinking strange and mysterious things happened in that building.

They didn't have a piano. Right there was enough to set them apart from the rest of us. At our church, if Elle May

Campbell wasn't banging away at the piano, most of us would have been off key and musically dysfunctional.

But at the Church of Christ, they didn't believe in musical instruments. So all the music was started by this guy who would blow through a pitch pipe to set the key. Since no one in Frostbite seemed to have that particular talent, there was a man from Blytheville who came over every Sunday and pitched the pipe, or whatever it was called, for the morning service.

Charley Hudson, one of the guys in my class at school, and I went by the church one day and found a car out front. On the front seat of the car, there was a pitch pipe just sitting there.

"You think that belongs to the guy who sets the pitch for them Church of Christ singings?" Charley asks me.

"Looks like it to me, Hud."

"What do you say we put a little bubble gum in a few slots and see how the singing turns out next Sunday?"

So sneaking back into our sinful natures, we quietly opened the door and took the pitch pipe. It was round, about twice the size of a silver dollar, and had little holes around the outside marked with the different musical pitches such as C Major or D Minor. Well, wanting to leave them a few notes to pitch on Sunday, we just filled in every other note with a little bubble gum. Superman with full lungs couldn't have gotten a note through those holes. Then we put the pitch pipe back on the car seat and made our way on down the street.

We never got the whole story, but some said that the singing at the Church of Christ the next Sunday would have made the angel Gabriel laugh. Everybody was trying to find the pitch. To tell the truth, they were having more trouble than the New York Yankees finding one that anyone in the ballpark couldn't hit over the fence.

On Monday it was the talk of the town. On Monday afternoon, my grandmother sent word she wanted to see me. I always liked going to her house because she would usually give me a dollar. But today things looked pretty serious.

My grandmother was a good Methodist woman, but she wasn't one of those uppity ones. She just loved the Lord, believed in that sprinkling stuff, and wore a plain old cotton dress on Easter.

"Son, you hear about that mess they had across the street yesterday?" she asked as she pointed over to the Church of Christ building.

"Yes ma'am, I heard it was a real mess," and that was the truth.

"You have anything to do with that?"

Now you have to understand that Grandma knew everything in town. One time, she told Eva Blackwater that she was going to have a baby. Eva liked to have died since her husband was off fighting for liberty in Korea and had been gone from Frostbite for over a year and a half. Some said the baby looked a lot like my uncle, but we better not go into that. But the fact is, I knew right then that she knew I was in on that pitch-pipe stuffing activity.

"Yes ma'am, I guess you would have to say I did have a little to do with that. But it was Hud that supplied the bubble gum. I just sort of helped stuff the pipe, if you know what I mean."

Well she lit into me like a tick on a dog. She just might tell my mama and let her beat the devil out of me. Better still, she would tell Bro. Earl Lee and let him use me for sermon material some Sunday when he was preaching on hell. Lord, she just about scared me to death.

Then she decided we ought to pray for my forgiveness.

So we got down on our knees and I confessed my terrible bubble-gum sin while Grandma added a few other sins of mine that she knew about but had not up to that point brought into the discussion. Leave it said that I did a pretty good job of confessing because the last thing I wanted was Bro. Earl Lee on my tail.

Then we got up from our knees and just sat around for a little bit.

Then Grandma said, "Y'all really stuffed that pipe with bubble gum?"

"Yes, ma'am, I guess we did."

A little smile came across her lips. "You think they hit any wrong notes on Sunday?"

"Well, I reckon they probably had a little problem with 'What a Friend We Have in Jesus,'" I offered, but I wasn't sure if it was safe for me to smile yet.

"I heard 'em all the way over here at my house," she grinned. "Sounded like a bunch of chickens trying to lay eggs."

"Yes, ma'am," and with that I just had to bust out laughing. But best of all was the fact that Grandma was laughing too. Tears were running down her eyes and, Lord knows, I thought she was gonna choke.

"Now, son," she said between howls, "I don't ever want to hear of you doing anything like that again. You hear me?" And then she almost fell off the chair again as howls of laughter rang through the house.

When we had finally composed ourselves, she brought out the cookies and a Coke and we just sat there grinning. When it was time to go, she handed me a rolled up bill that I always knew was the dollar she had for me.

I tell you, I was some kind of surprised when on the way home I unrolled that dollar and found out it was a big fiver. About then, I quit worrying about Bro. Earl Lee.

All in all, the Church of Christ folks were probably pretty good people. We didn't know much about them, but they didn't cause any harm and usually went straight home from their service so we didn't have to hassle with them at the BBQ place.

• • •

Then there was the church out behind Mr. R.C.'s store, the First Baptist Church. Just the name itself had been a matter of controversy for years and years. You see, this church was the black folks' church and most of the white Baptists were really ticked that they had missed out on getting to name their church the First Baptist Church. You will remember that the black folks had already taken that name. That did not set well with the good white Baptists who, under protest, had to worship at the Frostbite Baptist Church.

But if you want me to be honest, I would have traded Bro. Earl Lee in a wink just to have been able to listen to the Rev. and Most Holy and Apostolic Moses R. Johnson. Now that man could preach! He had been pastor of the First Baptist Church for as long as anyone could remember.

The interesting thing about the Rev. and Most Holy and Apostolic Moses R. Johnson was that during the week, he sacked groceries down at Mr. R.C's grocery store and everyone, except my brother and me, called him Moses. We called him Mr. Moses like Mama taught us. If we hadn't she would have killed us; however, that is another story. But on Sunday that man did go through a transformation.

I can see him now. Here he comes down the street on Sunday morning. Always that same black long-tail suit with his white tie, white handkerchief in the pocket, and his black shiny shoes covered with white spats. That man was something to see.

And Lord, could he preach. As I was a member of the Frostbite Baptist Church, you may find yourself wondering how I know that the Rev. and Most Holy and Apostolic Moses R. Johnson could preach. Well it is a long story ... but I will try to make it short for you ... which will not be easy to do.

One summer my daddy, Bro. Earl Lee, and four other upstanding deacons at the Frostbite Baptist Church decided to pay a visit to Moses and talk him into changing the name of his church. So they all went down, I believe it was, on a Wednesday afternoon because Baptists find their most religious times to be Sunday morning and Wednesday evening. But anyway, they went down to the store to talk to Moses — that's what they called him during the week. On Sunday, they called him *Rev.* Moses. That was about as close to the Rev. and Most Holy and Apostolic Moses R. Johnson as they wanted to get.

Well, Moses wasn't in any mood to change the name of his church. Frankly, he was drawing a bigger crowd than Bro. Earl Lee and I think he thought he sort of had the upper hand. Well, it was finally decided that Moses and Bro. Earl Lee would each go to the other's Sunday service and talk to the congregation about the name change. Right there shows how desperate the Frostbite Baptist Church folks were because if they weren't under the gun, you would not have found them within 100 yards of a black church on Sunday morning. And some of the founders — my granddaddy included — would be spinning in their graves to know that a black preacher was going to preach to the white folks at the church they had started.

But anyway, the time came for the pulpit exchange and Bro. Earl Lee went first. He got the Associational Missionary (about as close as Baptists come to having a Bishop) to come cover for him and on the given Sunday, he went down to preach to the black folks at the First Baptist Church to explain why we needed their name.

Daddy and the other four deacons went with Bro. Earl Lee. And because it was the first time I had ever begged to go to church, Daddy took me along. All the way over on the walk to the First Baptist Church, the deacons kept saying to Bro. Earl Lee, "Now, preacher, it is important that you don't preach on hell today. Just keep calm and tell them why the name of the churches should be changed." Bro. Earl Lee listened mainly because three of the five deacons were on the finance committee that set his salary, and there are just some things that even a man called of God won't mess with.

So the Rev. and Most Holy and Apostolic Moses R. Johnson, or Moses as we called him during the week, introduced Bro. Earl Lee and explained the nature of his coming even though everyone present knew why he was there. If I had to guess, I would have to say that the Rev. and Most Holy and Apostolic Moses R. Johnson took about 15 minutes in the introduction. He even called Bro. Earl Lee "Dr." Earl Lee, which was a real joke because we all knew Bro. Earl Lee wasn't even a registered nurse. You don't get many doctoral degrees in the third grade.

True to his word, Bro. Earl Lee kept it calm. He made the case using three points, two of which seemed to make sense to all us white representatives, but caught a little resistance among the black brothers and sisters. The third point none of us liked. If I remember correctly his three points went something like this:

1. The white folks needed to worship at the First Baptist Church because Jesus was white and would have wanted to be in the "first" church. After all, the Bible does say, "The first shall be first...." That is not exactly what it says, but at that moment that version seemed to best fit Bro. Earl Lee's needs.

II. The white folks needed to worship at the First Baptist Church because that was the way it was in every other city, town or village across this great nation. That was the American way. If the president, I think it was Harry Truman at the time, ever came to Frostbite, Arkansas, he would want to worship with the white people and would want to worship with them at the First Baptist Church. Changing the name was the *patriotic* thing to do. (He chose not to mention that the closest any president of these United States had ever come to Frostbite, Arkansas, was the time when Herbert Hoover made a trip to Memphis and then immediately threw the country into "one of them damn Republican depressions," as my daddy called it.)

And finally:

III. The white folks needed to worship at the First Baptist Church because if the name wasn't changed, he would do everything he could to calm the men of his church, but he would make no promises. Jobs could be lost, terrible things could happen in the name of the Lord, etc. Etc.

Well, we knew when he cut loose on that third point we were in trouble. Lord only knows the last thing we needed in Frostbite, Arkansas, was a race fight. But that was exactly what Bro. Earl Lee was promising. I saw my daddy and Mr. R.C. just slink down in their seats and hope we would all get out alive.

So in a few minutes, Bro. Earl Lee was finished with his calm, persuasive sermon and we got up to leave. You could have heard Miss Stella's lawn mower if she had been mowing that Sunday, which she usually did thus giving Bro. Earl Lee a major sin sermon about working on Sunday.

The next Sunday, Bro. Earl Lee told his congregation that he thought he had done a pretty good job and that the issue was closed, but in the nature of fair play he had invited Moses to come preach for us on the following Sunday. He didn't call him by his religious name of the Rev. and Most Holy and Apostolic Moses R. Johnson, primarily to show that this was just old Moses the grocery store sacker coming and that it might be worth coming next Sunday just to hear what he had to say.

That next Sunday, there had never been so many members at the Frostbite Baptist Church Sunday service. The attendance board indicated 85 in attendance, but some said there were well over a hundred. The offering was over $500 for the first time in 10 years. The Rev. and Most Holy and Apostolic Moses R. Johnson was there in all his Sunday splendor. He made Bro. Earl Lee look like a survivor from a refugee camp.

Bro. Earl Lee didn't waste any time with fancy introductions. "We got Moses here to talk to us for a few minutes about this name change that is about to take place. Get up here, Moses, and say what you have to say."

With great dignity, the Rev. and Most Holy and Apostolic Moses R. Johnson came to the pulpit. Later I asked Mama and Daddy exactly what Moses had said and they didn't rightly know. All we knew was that for almost two hours, the Rev. and Most Holy and Apostolic Moses R. Johnson cut loose with the Word like we had never heard of before or since. We thought Bro. Earl Lee could raise hell in the pulpit, but the Rev. and Most Holy and Apostolic Moses R. Johnson put Bro. Earl Lee to shame.

He walked with Jesus. "Say Amen!" That was a big line and before long those white Baptists were saying "Amen" and "Preach on Preacher" like they never had before. About half way through the service, Miss Stella, the spinster lady of Sunday lawn-mowing fame, cut loose shouting and came as close to speaking in tongues as you will ever hear in a Baptist church.

As best I can recall, the Rev. and Most Holy and Apostolic Moses R. Johnson never once mentioned the name change during his sermon. By the time he finished, those white Baptists were clapping and praising Jesus like never before or since. It was something to see and hear.

Then the Rev. and Most Holy and Apostolic Moses R. Johnson started to wind down:

Lord, You know we got a situation here. Say Amen!

And Lord, You know that what is, is, and don't need no tampering. Say Amen!

And Lord, You know Bro. Earl Lee may be the greatest preacher in the world and is known all over this country as the great pastor of the Frostbite Baptist Church. Say Amen!

And Lord, You know that if we change names then some of them peoples around the world are gonna think Bro. Earl Lee done gone and lost his mind and started pastoring a black church in Arkansas. Say Amen!

And Lord, You know we don't want him to bear that burden, not in these restless times. Say Amen!

So for the sake of Bro. Earl Lee and our love for him and the work he is doing for You, let's don't mess with them names. Say Amen!

Thank you folks for letting me come this morning and speaking my peace. Say Amen!

I'm gonna leave you now.

And with that he walked down the aisle to stunned silence. Not a word could be heard until finally Bro. Earl Lee got to his feet and walked up to that pulpit.

Two weeks ago, Bro. Earl Lee was ready to burn crosses, but suddenly Moses — better known at the First Baptist Church of Frostbite, Arkansas, as the Rev. and Most Holy and Apostolic Moses R. Johnson — had hit on a point that Bro. Earl Lee had not thought about. Lord only knew what would happen if word got out that Bro. Earl Lee had moved down to the black church to be its pastor.

Now Bro. Earl Lee may have been ignorant, but he was not stupid. The crowd was quiet as he started speaking:

Y'all know these are troubled times. There was a lynching over at Jonesboro just last month. Now we don't need that here in our town. We godly white folks have always treated our colored niggers with respect and kindness. And another thing, we are building a great church here, just look at the size of this congregation today. The last thing we need is to lose our momentum by fighting over this name change stuff. So I recommend we keep our name and let them folks keep theirs. Do I hear a motion to that effect?

Bro. Forsyth got up and made the motion as requested by the pastor. But before a vote could be taken, my daddy got up to amend the motion. Now there is something you need to know about Daddy. There wasn't a racist bone in his body. Because of that, he thought Bro. Earl Lee's actions down at the black church were about as shameful as a man of God could be. So he got up to amend the motion. And it went something like this:

"Bro. Earl Lee, I heard the motion and I think it should pass. But I would like to add an amendment to it."

"Go ahead, Bro. Elroy. What do you want to say in your amendment?"

"Well, Bro. Earl Lee, I make a motion we pass Bro. Forsyth's motion with the amendment being that at least once a quarter you have to ask the Rev. and Most Holy and Apostolic Moses R. Johnson to come back and preach for us."

With that the whole congregation clapped their hands and said, almost in unison, "Say Amen! Say Amen!"

The motion passed and Frostbite Baptist Church remained the citadel of white graciousness that everyone had known it to be all along. But best of all, once a quarter, the Rev. and Most Holy and Apostolic Moses R. Johnson came back and preached us to heaven like no other preacher had ever done. It was a fine outcome to what could have been a bad situation.

•••

Now, finally, we come to the Frostbite Baptist Church; the fourth and final citadel of spiritual warfare in this corner of Arkansas.

Everyone has his or her own special spiritual starting place. Jesus launched his unofficial ministry in the Temple when he was 12 years old and His "professional" ministry after His baptism by John the Baptist. Saul got started down the Lord's way on the road to Damascus and even changed his name to Paul. Moses got a good start on his work leading the children of Israel out of Egypt. And I got my start in the Frostbite Baptist Church in Frostbite, Arkansas.

It was in that church that I was "saved, sanctified and set apart!" It was right there on the front pew where Jimmy Allen almost stabbed me to death with his mama's fingernail file that I learned nonviolence. It was a time when my mama spanked me with a willow limb for not fighting back. Lord knows religion was confusing even back then!

It was in that church that Mr. Davis Love used to heist the tunes and where no one ever sang the third stanza of any gospel hymn.

It was in that church where Mr. Harlen Evans used to sing "The Ninety and Nine" and have the entire congregation in tears, either from sadness or from stifling a good laugh because old Mr. Evans never hit two notes on key.

And it was in that church that I learned about tithing. Tithing to a Baptist is like mud to a hog. You get in the habit of it and it just feels good. But ignore it and you knew that, once a year, Bro. Earl Lee was going to lay into you with the Word of the Lord about that tithing stuff. Now tithing to a Baptist meant giving 10 percent of your income to the church. There was always a lot of discussion on whether that was before or after taxes, but either way, those who practiced it felt a holy piousness about it.

At our house, Mama believed in tithing and Daddy believed in Mama, so we usually practiced it. In fact, from the time I can remember, Mama would give me a 25-cent weekly allowance and in the name of the Lord rip a nickel off it and make me put it in the offering plate. As best I can figure that was somewhat over the 10 percent requirement, but Mama was teaching me a lesson. That lesson was: You give or the Lord will get you! Say Amen!

On the other hand, my daddy spent a lot of time trying to figure out what the Lord really meant about this tithing stuff. We were a farm family. He borrowed to make the crop every year, and then paid off the loan when the crop came in. To my knowledge, in the 18 years I lived at home, the farm never made a profit. So as far as daddy was concerned, the tithe was irrelevant. But it was not so to Mama. Bless her heart, that woman did believe in that tithing stuff.

Every time something bad happened to someone, she would say, "I'll just bet you a pretty penny they stopped tithing and the Lord got 'em." That would set my daddy's argument back a few months, then we would be in debt again, and he would make his case for not having anything to give. But at the Frostbite Baptist Church, you were expected to give, so every week Mama would put a little something in the plate to keep us in good standing.

The Frostbite Baptist Church was a little yellow brick building across from the schoolyard. It had an auditorium that would seat about 150 people though, to my knowledge, the seats had never been used all at one time. Behind the auditorium, there were the Sunday school building and fellowship hall. A small kitchen served as the gathering place for many a homemade casserole to be served at special gatherings. Baptists will get up a crowd in a flash if home cooking is involved.

When the church was built, families could give an extra $150 and have a stained glassed window dedicated to a loved one. My granddaddy had died by the time I was old enough to read and one of the glasses was dedicated "In Memory of Sam Hamilton." Since I was named after him that sort of spooked me every time I looked up and saw a window with my name on it even if it was in memory of my granddaddy.

The church had a piano, which was never in tune, an electronic organ, and some shaped-note hymnbooks. And right in the center, the church had a baptistery that was really just a big tub of water where Bro. Earl Lee would dunk the new believers. One of the good things about being saved in the Frostbite Baptist Church was the strong belief in "once saved, always saved." That just meant that once you had accepted the Lord, been baptized in His name and had your name written in the Book by some angel up in heaven, it could never be erased. I have to tell you that in my later years when I drifted a little bit, that one thing right there was a real comfort. Mama kept telling me that my salvation probably didn't take, but I trusted in old Bro. Earl Lee's "once saved, always saved" teaching.

In the Baptist church, the congregation gets to select its own pastor. This is described as "calling a new pastor," which in laymen's terms means just going out and trying to get someone else's pastor so that church will then call someone else's pastor ... and around and around it goes.

I was just about eight years old when our church called Bro. Earl Lee. The one thing I remember about that event was that he came out to our house for Sunday dinner on his first Sunday as the new preacher. He had preached until about 1 o'clock and it was hot and he was all sweaty, but we were honored to have him at our table just the same. Man, could that preacher eat. What I remember most about that meal was when my daddy, who was always a little skeptical of any new preacher, said to Bro. Earl Lee. "Preacher, what exactly caused you to accept the call to our little church? It ain't exactly big-time around here."

"Well," said Bro. Earl Lee, "over there in Lone Oak where I was preaching, they was paying me $25 a week. Frankly, Bro. Elroy, when I heard that the Frostbite Baptist Church was paying $50 a week, it ceased to be a call and it became a holler!" Then Bro. Earl Lee burst out laughing. You could have heard him halfway back to Frostbite, which was a good two-mile walk up the road.

My daddy picked up the cornbread and passed it to Bro. Earl Lee and said, "Here Earl Lee, have some more cornbread. You may be the first honest preacher I have ever met!" And a long friendship was begun from that day until death did them part. My daddy also pointed out that, in his long affiliation with the Baptist church, he had never heard of a preacher being called to a church that paid less than where he was presently serving. Bro. Earl Lee's honesty gave my daddy ammunition for his arguments on that subject for years to come.

It was in the Frostbite Baptist Church that someone heard my call into the ministry. It was here that I was ordained and had 40 preachers from all over the county come to lay hands on me. It was here that I preached my first sermon: a real masterpiece on hell. I was going along fine until I used an illustration about Noah and the whale, which most enjoyed until someone pointed out to me that it was Jonah and the whale. But that experience taught me early on that most people didn't really listen to what you said anyway.

Frostbite Baptist Church could be a loving church family and it could be as mean a group as you had ever wanted to meet. When my mama and daddy had their 50th wedding anniversary, the church honored them with "Martha and Elroy Day" and all their children and grandchildren came home to share that special moment. But this was also the same congregation that ostracized my mama and daddy because one harvest season they invited the Mexican missionary, who came in to minister to the migrant workers during harvest, to stay at their house. For that racial indiscretion they were shunned and no one spoke to them for almost two years.

So what I am saying is, it was just a church made up of people. Some good and some not so good. Some who prayed too long and some who didn't know how to pray. But when trouble came along, they stood together. When I was 10, our house burned down. The next week the people of the town came together and had a shower for us at the high school auditorium. In less than two hours, they had furnished a new house for us and raised over a thousand dollars to help us get started again. And at that school that night there were Methodist, Frostbite Baptist, Church of Christ and First Baptist folks all present just taking care of people they loved.

So as I look back on it, maybe Bro. B.J. Forsyth's prayers were not so long, maybe not even long enough. And maybe the Methodist folks were not so uppity. Maybe those Church of Christ folks weren't as strange as Charley Hudson and I thought they were. And maybe, just maybe, the Rev. and Most Holy and Apostolic Moses R. Johnson walked closer to Jesus than any of us.

Five

Old Moses — not the Rev. and Most Holy and Apostolic Moses R. Johnson of Frostbite, Arkansas, but the real Moses of the Bible — was walking down the road one day and he saw this bush up on the hillside. Thinking a real brush fire might break out and the National Guard might have to be called up to put out the brush fire, Moses went up to check it out. When he got there, he saw this one bush that was just burning like mad and didn't seem to be a threat to anything, so he just stood there looking at it.

Then all at once, that bush started to talk to him.

Now I had an uncle who spent a lot of time talking to a tree out behind his house in Frostbite, Arkansas, but he also spent a lot of time drinking moonshine whiskey. So when I first heard the story of Moses, I wasn't too surprised. To a little kid, there was a strong similarity to the two personalities.

But anyway, this voice in the bush was the voice of God telling old Moses it was time for him to get busy and go lead the children of Israel out of Egypt. I bring this up because it was one of the first recorded times of a call to the ministry. From that point on, a lot of people stood around looking for burning bushes to tell them how to serve the Lord when what they really needed to do was just get up off their sorry behinds and go do something to spread the Word.

In Frostbite, Arkansas, there was a more formalized way whereby a young man received his calling into the ministry. Since this was flat, Mississippi Delta country and every spare acre of land was cultivated for cotton farming, there just weren't many bushes standing around to become calling spots.

I don't know how the other churches did it, but at the Frostbite Baptist Church there were five spiritual giants of the church who usually made up the calling committee. For as long as anyone could remember, this calling tradition of using five elders of the church went back at least four generations before I came along. So by my time this was pretty well the way you got nailed, excuse me I meant to say called, into the Baptist ministry in Frostbite, Arkansas.

Here is the way it would work. The five elders of the church would watch the crowd of young people. If they found someone who looked promising, they would pay the target a visit. At that visit, they would tell him (in that day even God was not radical enough to call a girl person to the preaching ministry in Frostbite, Arkansas) the Lord sent them to notify the young man that he was being called into the ministry. This was not a free and open discussion, it was pretty much what one might call a dictated vocation.

After talking with my grandma, I could go back a long way and trace the history, but let me just begin with my father. When I speak of my daddy I am really talking about my stepfather who married my mama after my real daddy died when I was four years old. My "real daddy" is the one I am referring to when I write about my daddy being called by the five elders. I know it gets confusing, but you should have tried to live through it.

When my daddy was 14 years old, the Elders came to him and told him he was called to preach the Word of the Lord from city to city which, in and of itself, was a little strange because the closest city to Frostbite of any size was Memphis, Tennessee, and my daddy had never been that far from home. But the fact is, this calling stuff was not something to mess with. So my daddy jumped in with both feet and started preaching the Word. From what I have heard, he was a real hellfire-and-damnation sort of preacher, a whole lot like Bro. Earl Lee.

But I have to tell you, there is a big difference in being called by the Elders and being called by the Lord through a burning bush. So try though he might, my daddy just never got into the hang of being a preacher. Oh, he did a great job when he was doing it. In fact, he started three churches during his short ministry and those three churches are still going strong today. But from what I hear, all he ever really wanted to do was come home and farm with his daddy, my grandpa, but that becomes a problem when you are under the gun, I meant to say call.

My daddy was 20 when my oldest brother, Danny, was born. At that time he had been preaching for six years. So about six years later, when I was born, he was 26 and had been preaching for 12 years. My daddy was making $25 dollars a week and listening to Mama cry silently in their bed at night because there wasn't any food in the house. The story is told of one really bad period when they were just about out of food. My daddy got on his knees in the living room and was praying for the Lord to send them something to eat when one of his buddies heard him praying — it was summer and the front door was open. His friend went to the store, bought a loaf of bread, then sneaked up to the front door of our house, threw the loaf as hard as he could, and hit my daddy in the back of the head.

My mama said that my daddy never paused, he just continued his prayer, "Thank you, Lord. Thank you, Jesus. I prayed for bread and you sent it. Yes, Jesus, the Lord sent us bread, but the devil brought it. Say Amen! and thank you, Jesus."

Those were tough times for this young father of two who was in the ministry because of a call from the Elders rather than a call from God. As I would learn later in my life, that is a burden that weighs heavily on the soul.

One day my daddy just gave up. He decided not to play out the charade any longer. So he and Mama moved back in with my grandpa and grandma and started over. He was now a farmer. He was no longer a preacher, but the demons of a false calling continued to haunt him. Having the Hamilton genes that caused a slight tilt toward devil rum, he took up drinking.

On a sunny day in April, after a night out with the boys and 16 years after the Elders had issued their call, my daddy was standing in the cotton field by a tractor and fell over dead. He as almost 30 years old.

And the town mourned his loss. And the Baptists said with great sincerity, "Well, he left his call and God got him. Thus is the way of the Lord."

Over the next six years, my mama farmed, moved us to Phoenix, Arizona, to see if the dry weather would cure my asthma, moved us back to Arkansas when Arizona didn't seem to make my health any better, and finally farmed again until she was on the brink of bankruptcy.

When she was about at the end of her financial rope, she signed to borrow $2,500 from Mr. Bert Ledbetter to make the crop. She mortgaged two mules, a planter, a plow, a singletree, and the proceeds of the crop. That year she planted the seed and then watched the rain start. We never got back in the field to harvest anything. As a result, the farm was about to be lost to Mr. Ledbetter. Mr. Ledbetter was a fine man, but he was also a businessman. And business was business.

But just like Superman from a phone booth, in came Elroy Hamilton to the rescue. A bachelor for 40 years, he married my mama, a woman with two sons, a big mortgage, and not many prospects for things to get any better.

He said, "Will you?" and my mama said, "Not only will I, but Mr. Bert Ledbetter will give me away!"

It was a great ceremony in our living room and in the blink of an eye, I had me a daddy. He didn't drink and he didn't preach. He was just a farmer with a third-grade education who loved the Lord and taught me more about integrity than any man I have ever known. Just to make things even around the house, Danny and I took the Hamilton name too. We were to all be in this thing together.

• • •

And on the day the Elders came to see me, it was my daddy, Elroy Hamilton, who alone took me aside and said, "Son, this preaching stuff is pretty heavy stuff so don't do it unless you know the Lord is in it."

That day, the day of the visit from the Elders, is not very clear in my mind today. It probably should be because it dictated my life's path for the next 20 years. I remember coming home from school one Monday afternoon to find the Elders in our living room. I was 14 years old, just like my real daddy had been.

There were five of them. There was Mr. Densmore, he was a drug store owner with a long beard. There was Mr. Johnson, he taught speech at the high school, which was pretty funny because he stuttered really bad. There was Mr. Forsyth, he often led us in prayer. There was Joe Taylor, he drove a gravel truck for the county. And finally, there was Bro. Earl Lee. The pastor of the church was always counted among the group of five.

As I recall, my daddy didn't seem real joyous as he pushed me into the living room, "Come in here, boy. These here men from the church want to have a little talk with you."

Bro. Earl Lee started the conversation, "Boy, I reckon you know why we are here. Me and these great men of God have come to talk to you about going into the ministry. We believe the Lord has laid His hand on you, and it is time you took up the sword of the Lord and started fighting the good fight for Jesus."

Mr. Densmore broke in. He was stroking his long black beard and he talked in a quiet whispery sort of voice, "Son, I been a watching you and the Lord's got His hand on you. Now I know this might be a shock to you, but we done prayed this through and the Lord has told us to come here and get you on down the road. Ain't that right, Bro. Johnson?"

Well Mr. Johnson, or Bro. Johnson as he was called on this day, started trying to say his peace. I knew when he started he was in trouble, and I was gonna be pretty soon if he kept it up. "S-S-S-Son," he said as he finally got it in gear, "y-y-you know know th-th-that this so-so-sorry world needs needs needs some-some-some-some*one* to tell te-te-tell them about J-J-Jesus. Well, you're i-i-it."

I looked over at Daddy and could see he was about to bust out laughing. I looked at Mama and she was in kind of a prayerful state. It just seemed to me I should look like Mama and I tried to stifle the laugh I was feeling. I prayed without even moving my lips, "Lord, if Mr. Johnson tries to say another word, I swear I can't hold it in no more so please let him stop right now." Right about then I was wishing for Moses' burning bush. I doubt the Lord Almighty stuttered even when talking through a burning bush.

But before I could pray one more sentence, Bro. Earl Lee had us all down on our knees on the floor and had just called on Bro. B.J. Forsyth to pray. We knew we were in for about 10 minutes of fighting the godless Communists and such, and personally I was about to die — I had to go pee. I looked at my daddy with a pained look on my face, but he had laid flat on the floor. Most folks would have thought he was prostrate before the Lord. I knew him well enough to know that he was thinking that if old B.J. was going to pray, he might as well get him a nap. But I was just about to have a holy accident.

Finally when I couldn't hold it any more, I jumped up and ran into the bathroom. I started to get a little of the physical pressure off my body while, out in the living room, the spiritual pressure was getting pretty heavy.

I listened as Bro. Forsyth wrapped up his talk with the Lord and everybody started standing up.

"Where'd the boy go?"

"H-h-he was h-here here when when we started to pr-pr-pr-pray."

Then I heard my daddy's voice, "I think the boy went to the bathroom."

Then Mama's voice: "He ain't been feeling real good the last day or two. This might just be a good time to leave him be for a little so he can think this through."

Then Bro. Earl Lee, "Ain't nothing to think about. The Lord has called and we have delivered the message. We'll just wait until he comes out and start taking the next step."

I sat down on the bathroom floor and thought I could wait them out. But about five minutes later, I heard my daddy knock on the door. "Son, come on out now. These men got a few more things to say to you and then we will have a little talk amongst ourselves."

So I opened the door and walked back into the living room to face God's messengers.

Bro. Earl Lee decided to wrap things up: "Boy, God's gonna do something with you. All's you gotta do is walk in His way and preach the Word. You ain't never gonna be rich in the way the world counts things, but you gonna be rich in spiritual things. So God bless you and by the way, you are gonna preach your first sermon Sunday morning so start getting ready. And another thing, don't go preach one of them Methodist sermonettes. Boy, you are a Baptist so preach like one. I expect about 45 minutes of hard preaching. You be sweating when you're though. You hear me?"

And with that they turned to leave. The only thing I remember happening after they stepped off the porch was my mama lifting her apron to her eyes to wipe away the tears that started to fall and my daddy picking up his hat and walking out the back door. Under his breath, I heard him make a four-letter word into three distinct syllables. "Sh-i-t" was the last word I heard as he stepped off the back porch and went to the barn.

Six

One thing that made no difference at all in preaching at the Frostbite Baptist Church was the need for deep theological thought. In fact, a few years later when I decided to go to college, the five elders paid another visit to try and talk me out of it. Their premise was that any preacher worth his salt ought to be able to get a message from God and preach it, and the only thing education could do was mess up the system. It is my distinct opinion that, as my life unfolded, the five elders would attest to the validity of their observations.

Whatever the case, I awakened on Wednesday morning with the cold realization that on Sunday I would be preaching my first sermon. I must admit, I knew little about the Bible except for the fact that the shortest verse in the Bible is John 11:35, "Jesus wept." I memorized that one so I would have a verse to quote in Sunday school when we were asked to name our favorite verse.

Now John 11:35 is a fine verse, but there was about a zero probability of getting a 45-minute sermon out of those two words. However, I do remember the time when Bro. Earl Lee used that verse for one of his sermons. If memory served, he went on for about two hours, so there was probably more there than met my eye.

But anyway, I was in a frenzy trying to come up with a sermon. Not only had I never prepared one, if the truth were known, I never listened to very many either. That is not to say I was not been present when sermons were preached, but counting the ceiling tiles and other such activities usually occupied my mind instead.

My only hope seemed to be Leroy Evers, who like myself, was 14 years old. The only difference between Leroy and me was that Leroy was a student of the Bible. He had great plans to be a Methodist bishop or some such lofty position someday, but the fact is Leroy was a bishop by the time he was six years old. I would say Leroy weighed about 100 pounds, stood 5'11" and had not started to shave. However, his voice was in the changing mode and would very often flop through about six octaves in a single sentence. If I was one to tell the truth, I would have to admit that because of his religious leanings, most of us stayed away from Leroy. That boy was some kind of serious about religion.

There was no doubt about it, Leroy was what you might call "different." That boy could whip out his Bible and lay a Scripture on you faster than Charley Hudson could get to the punch line of a dirty joke. Most of us were not really into Scripture-laying during our high school days.

Also, Leroy could quote verses that most of us had never heard before or since. He knew that Abraham's wife, Sarah, had a name change when she married Abraham. She changed her name from Sarai to Sarah and, for some reason, that was a big deal to Leroy. Always said he was going to find someone named Sarai to marry just to see if she would get a message from God to change her name to Sarah also. The fact is, he married Ruby Tuttle because they were about to "begot" a child if you know what I mean.

Though I would not have been caught dead with old Leroy except in times of dire desperation, I found myself in such a time and sought him out. Leroy was president of the MYF. Therefore, most of his free time was spent down at the Methodist church. So off I went to that uppity church to find Leroy. But instead of Leroy, who should be there but Bro. Webb eating a spam sandwich made from a whole can of spam and two slices of bread that were spread with home-churned butter.

Fighting the urge to throw up, I asked, "Bro. Webb, you seen Leroy around this afternoon?"

"He was here a little earlier, but he left after putting up the decorations for the dance Friday night. I don't know where he went." He said that without ever pausing in his eating. How he could do that was the subject of much speculation around town.

Right there I knew I was in trouble. If Bro. Earl Lee saw me down here at the Methodist church when they were putting up decorations for a dance, my preaching career would be the shortest in history. But since I was there, I decided to do a little theological research.

"Bro. Webb, how come Methodists can dance and Baptists can't?" I could tell by his look that was the first serious theological question he had faced in a while.

Wiping the spam juice on his sleeve he replied, "'Cause us Methodists ain't got no Earl Lee preaching to us. Ain't nothing wrong with a little dancing. Look in the Bible boy, you gonna find God's people dancing all over the place."

"Then how come Bro. Earl Lee is so hard against it?"

And Bro. Webb so kindly explained, "Well, boy, when God was putting all his people together, he made some mighty strange ones. In my humble opinion, Baptists are amongst some of the strangest. And right at the top of the heap is your Bro. Earl Lee. He don't know no better 'cause he was raised to believe that dancing is bad. So now he is teaching the next generation of you Baptist kids that it is bad. And then you will do the same and it will just never end. Best thing you can do is just preach to get people into the pearly gates and let the Lord worry about the dancing part."

This was about the longest I had ever talked to a Methodist preacher in my life so I decided to make the best of it. Seemed as if Bro. Webb had some common sense about him and might be able to give me some pointers about the forthcoming sermon disaster that was fast-approaching in about four days. So with plagiarism in mind, I asked, "Bro. Webb, tell me about your first sermon. Were you scared like I am? How old were you? Who told you that the calling was on you?"

And Bro. Webb kindly looked up from his meal, guess this might take a while. "Whoa, boy, slow down a little. You asking a mighty lot of questions there. Let's start with that last one. The Lord called me Hisself. Now I didn't see no burning bush, nothing like that. But one day when the preacher was preaching on serving the Lord, I just knew that was what the Lord wanted me to do. Sort of hard to explain, but ain't never been no doubt the Lord called me.

"I preached my first sermon one week after my 25th birthday, and yes, I was as scared as you are or worse. By that time, I had a wife and a baby and here I was about to send us into the Lord's work with no visible means of income. You bet I was scared. But all in all it turned out all right. You have to remember that Methodists don't require a lot."

I just needed a place to start. "What'd you preach about?"

"'Bout 15 minutes," and he let out a laugh that could have been heard all the way down at Mr. R.C.'s store. "Yes, sir, boy, let me tell you. If you want to make it as a preacher, just don't ever run past 15 minutes and they will love you till you die. Now get out of here and go work on your 15 minutes for Sunday. I may just shut this place down early and let all us Methodists come hear you."

I did not find a lot of comfort in that statement. In fact, I left Bro. Webb's office with a real burden on my heart. I thought preaching was about getting people saved and such, but he seemed to think it was about getting it over in a hurry. Somehow it just didn't all fit in my way of thinking. I really needed to talk to Leroy.

I walked on down toward the school house. The school was about three blocks from the Methodist church, and I knew every person who lived in the houses along the way. Fortunately none of them were out on their front porch so I didn't have to make small talk and answer questions about my up-and-coming preaching debut. Sure enough, I spotted Leroy sitting under the pecan tree on the school yard. Sensing my intense desperation, Leroy motioned for me to come on over. He had heard about my calling and just wanted me to know that he was praying the Lord would be with me. He didn't say that with one of them sly grins everyone else was giving me. Sounded to me like he meant it. I decided it was time we got down to some serious talking.

"Leroy, I got a sermon to preach on Sunday, and I don't know how to put together no sermon, much less preach one. How about you help me put together something?"

"Think them Baptists can use a Methodist sermon?" he asked with that little crooked smile that seemed to work on all the teachers.

"You work it up, and I'll baptize it for the Baptists." We both laughed and I was deciding ol' Leroy might come in handy after all.

"Well," he asked, "do you want it to be topical or exegetical?"

"Hell, Leroy, I don't even know what them words mean. I just want to get it over in about 15 minutes or less and then go home."

Then he spoke with authority, "Sounds like topical is gonna work best for you. A topical sermon is where you preach on a topic in the Bible rather than taking a verse and going into the Greek or Hebrew meaning. That is called exegetical. Now, if it is going to be topical, you gotta decide on a topic. You could preach on sin: Baptists seem real big on that one. You could preach on love: the girls will think you are mighty sensitive and would be all over you. You could preach on heaven: the old folks will smile and feel good 'cause they're 'bout to go there. So you just gotta decide who you want to impress. It is real hard to hit everyone with a topical sermon."

I sat there thinking that I was really in over my head. But Bro. Earl Lee seemed to be big on hell so I decided to go in that direction. "Leroy, seems to me like my first sermon ought to be on hell. What you know about hell?"

"Well, I know if you are going to preach you need an outline. You need at least three points. And if you were gonna preach a Methodist sermon, it would be real good to have a poem, but I don't think you Baptists are very big on poems, so let's just stick to the points. What text do you want to use?"

"What's a text?"

"Good Lord Almighty! You don't even know what a text is? Man, we got our work cut out. A text is the verse of Scripture you want to use when you preach on hell. Now what do you say? Which one you want to use?"

I racked my brain and could not come up with any Scripture 'cept "Jesus wept" and somehow I didn't think that was going to do it. "Leroy, what if we get our three points and then find a Scripture to back it up?" I was later to find that a lot of preachers worked it out in that reverse direction.

"I don't think that's what you are supposed to do, but let's try it. Now we need a sermon title so you can say, 'Today I am going to preach to you on' and then name the subject. Now we know you are going to preach on hell, but that is a little strong so you need to cover it up and then hit them with the hell stuff. What about this? 'Life without God.' What you think about that?"

"Sounds good to me. You got any points to go with it?" Maybe he could put this thing together for me.

Leroy took out his tablet and a pencil and went to work. In a few minutes, he handed me a sheet of paper and asked me what I thought about it. On it was written:

Point #1
Life without God is a hell of a way to live.

Point #2
Life without God is a hell of a way to die.

Point #3
Life without God is a hell of a way to spend eternity.

Looked pretty good to me. So after thanking Leroy for his help, I hurried off to prepare my 15-minute sermon for the coming Sunday morning. I was ready to "cut wood" as Bro. Earl Lee would say.

I timed the three points. Only 14 minutes and 30 seconds to go. I was feeling pretty good.

The only thing really bothering me was finding a verse of Scripture to back all these "hell" points up. As I said before, me and the Bible were sort of strangers up to this point. As I was walking home from the school yard where Leroy had implanted this fine sermon outline in my head, I passed Elle May Campbell's house and nearly jumped out of my skin when she called my name. She had been sitting in her rocker out in the front yard under the big cottonwood tree and I just plain did not seen her. I thought for sure I was finally hearing the voice of God.

"Come here, boy. Yo grandma tells me you gonna be preaching to us on Sunday. Is at true?"

"Yes, ma'am. Looks like you gonna have to listen to me, Miss Elle. Bro. Earl Lee says he's gonna step aside and let me lay into y'all this Sunday. You gonna be there playing the piano to get them warmed up for me?"

"Boy, I wouldn't miss it. I heard your daddy preach his first sermon. I had just started playing the piano at the church and he was preaching his first sermon. Funniest sermon I ever heard. Lord, to this day when I think about it, I nearly bust out laughing. That boy tried to preach on hell and he got it so screwed up most of us were not sure whether we were supposed to go to hell or heaven. This here whole town laughed about it for years. By the way, what you gonna be preaching about?"

"I'm sort of still working on it." I wasn't about to tell her my outline for my sermon on hell. Sounded like my daddy had about covered that subject.

"Well, you better get on out of here and get to work on it. I expect to hear a mighty fine sermon Sunday so don't let me down. By the way, boy. I'm gonna be praying for you. I s'pect you gonna be in need of a little prayer support."

If I felt higher than a kite after talking to Leroy, I felt lower than a snake after talking to Miss Elle. Here I was with the only outline in my whole sermon file being one on the same subject that my daddy had preached on some 26 years before and they were still laughing about it. Suddenly the day looked gray and dismal and Sunday loomed before me like a spiritual monster that would ruin my life for good.

Just up the street where I was walking I could see Bro. Earl Lee's car parked at the church so I decided to stop in and see if I could get any relief from him. If nothing else, I believed Bro. Earl Lee was close to the Lord and he might help me come up with another outline for Sunday.

The door of the church was unlocked as always. The fact is, most doors in Frostbite stayed unlocked. Or if someone did lock the door, he was usually kind enough to tack a note on the door that told everyone where the key was hidden. Here at the church I don't think anyone had a key so the door was never locked. Bro. Earl Lee said they left it open just in case some poor lost sinner needed to come to the altar to pray. And right about now I was feeling like I needed to pray, so I opened the door and went on in.

It was dark. I don't know why churches have to always be dark in the middle of the day, but Frostbite Baptist Church was dark inside so I had to let my eyes adjust before walking on in to look for Bro. Earl Lee. No more than had my eyes adjusted till I saw somebody on his knees at the altar. There was a low moaning sound coming from up there and there was a groaning that made the whole place sound like Turnip Allen's house on Halloween night. Turnip's folks were big into Halloween and some folks said they worshipped the devil, but that's for another time.

As I got closer I could tell it was Bro. Earl Lee and he was doing what was called "groaning in the spirit." That was just a Baptist way of saying he was praying and about every third sentence he would moan a little and say something like "Please, Jesus let it be. Amen and amen!"

If you have never heard someone groan in the spirit, you have missed one of the more memorable moments of your spiritual journey. That is especially true if you are in bad need for a sermon on Sunday and think a little groaning might help you too.

I just slipped in a pew about halfway back from the altar where Bro. Earl Lee was praying and tried to be respectful.

I figured he'd get over this moaning and groaning in a few minutes and I would talk to him about my sermon, or lack thereof.

Sure enough, after about five minutes, he stopped his praying. With his hand on the communion table, he pushed himself up. Looked as if that praying stuff had sort of stiffened up his knees a little, but as he slowly got everything back in the right place he turned and look straight at me.

"Well, well," he said "If it ain't the next Billy Sunday."

Since Billy Sunday had been one of the great evangelists of years past, I figured that was a compliment. But the way Bro. Earl Lee said it, I wasn't for sure. I ignored it and moved on to why I was there, "Bro. Earl Lee, I got me a sermon outline for Sunday and I thought you might just look it over and give me your impression."

"Boy, did the Lord give you that sermon?"

Sometimes I thought I just ought to change my name to "boy" because it seemed like everyone in town called me that. But this weren't no time to be arguing about a name since Sunday was moving up pretty fast.

"Well, He gave it to me, but He might have used someone to deliver it."

I could tell right off that Bro. Earl Lee thought I was talking about him. "Well, boy, if you got a little something from me or someone else I guess that is all right. Don't give me the whole nine yards. Just tell me what you gonna preach about."

"I'm aimin' on preaching about hell."

He jumped straight up and clapped his hands, "Lord, God Almighty, we got us a preacher here! Yes, sir, you preach on hell for your first sermon and we will know right off the Lord's got His hand on you. Ain't nothing the Lord likes better than a little hell-raising in the pulpit. Now you go on and work on that sermon. I got a feeling the Lord is really gonna turn you on, boy." With that, he headed for the door like he was going to a fire.

I guess I was looking for a little more help than what he had given me, but it was too late now. Right now, I just decided to take Leroy's outline and put as much meat on it as I could and lay the wood to the fire on Sunday morning.

Seven

THE NEXT FEW DAYS WERE pretty tense around the house. Daddy didn't say much. He never was a talker, but it seemed as if he was less than quiet since the Elders had come by. Even that lame brain brother of mine kept his mouth shut. Mama seemed to want to talk about things, but not getting much of a response from anyone, she pretty much stopped talking too.

By Thursday the tension was pretty high. About two that afternoon I came home and Mama was sitting at the big round table in the kitchen snapping beans for supper. Usually when I would find her this way, she would be humming a gospel song or something. But today, just like the day before, she just sat there thinking. I decided this was as good a time as any to get some talking done.

"Mama, you think we could do a little talking about them men that came over to the house on Monday." It wasn't like I had to explain. That visit had been on everyone's mind for the past three days.

Mama got up from the table and took the beans she had been working on over to the sink. She seemed to take her time washing them again, then she got out a big pot, filled it with water and put the beans in it. They needed to soak a while before she would throw the bacon fat in the pot and cook them for supper. I had watched this ritual a hundred times.

Then she wiped her hands on her apron and turned back to me. "Want some milk or something? Maybe a soda?"

"No, ma'am. Guess I just want to talk."

As she was known to do, she walked by my chair and rubbed my head before she pulled up a chair sort of in front of mine, just the rounding of the table between us. "Well?"

And so I started, "Mama, do you believe them Elders were told by God that I'm supposed to be a preacher?"

She waited a long time before she answered. I could tell she was struggling with what to say. "Son, I just don't know. You know your real daddy went through this same thing and you see where it got him. I never did know whether God called him or whether the Elders back then did, but I sure know it didn't take, whoever did the calling.

"I been giving this a lot of thought since Monday. I done a lot of reading in my Bible since then. I guess after reading up on it some, I would have to say God does call folks to preach the Word. Lord knows we would be in a mess if He didn't. I just don't find no place where the calling went through somebody else to get to them. You know what I mean?"

I could see she was struggling with this. I knew I was. "Yes, ma'am, I know what you mean. Seems like there is a lot in the Bible about folks hearing the voice of God even about ordinary things. Mama, you ever heard the voice of God?"

She answered, "No, not really. I guess I mostly just had to take some of this stuff by faith, 'cause I never did hear any voices, that's for sure."

"Mama, I'm scared. I don't want to be no preacher unless the Lord calls me and at this point, I sure ain't heard nothing out of the ordinary. What if I don't get no calling? What if them Elders were wrong and I take off preaching and God ain't behind it? What then?"

"Son, I don't have any answers for you. Maybe you ought to just start down that road and see what the Lord does with you. You won't be the first 14-year-old preaching wonder that ever hit the county." She paused and neither of us said anything for a minute or two. Then she continued, "You done any getting ready for your sermon on Sunday?"

"I mostly been worried about the call."

Then she told me the news. "Well you might want to get started on something. Up at the post office this morning, I saw a sign Bro. Earl Lee had put up inviting everybody in town to come hear you preach on Sunday. Guess you better try to get this one out of the way since it is already being talked about."

Then she did something that I wasn't accustomed to Mama doing. She reached over and rubbed my head again, then stood up and just pressed my head into herself like she thought I was going to run away or something. Then without a word she just went to her bedroom and closed the door.

•••

My biggest fear was having to get up in front of all those people and talk. Last year, we sent Jerry Stillman from our high school down to Little Rock to the National Beta Club convention. We were running him for state president and he was supposed to get up and make a speech telling everyone why they should vote for him.

Most of us felt that once he drove up in that new MG automobile, he was a sure thing to get the cheerleader vote. Before driving to Little Rock, he had seen that the steering wheel had been put back on real tight and had asked Bro. Webb to refrain from sitting in the driver's seat. We pretty much thought he was a shoo-in.

Jerry did pretty good until they introduced him. He stood up and saw all those people out there waiting on him to say something important. He stammered a few words and staggered back to his seat. I think the vote was 512 to 4, against him. Thank the Lord our school had four votes or it would have been a complete shut-out.

I guess my biggest fear the first time I would see my own crowd waiting on me to say something important was that I would turn out like Jerry.

During my high school years, I made a little room for myself. Our house wasn't very big so, to get a little privacy, you pretty much had to be creative. The room I built was up in the attic. I put some flooring down, ran a light over to a cot so I could see to read, set up my record player, and moved in. I could pull the stairs down, go up to my room, pull the stairs back up, and I would be in a world of my own. Maybe it was Jerry I was thinking about as I pulled the stairs down to go up to my room that day. If I didn't want to make a fool of myself like he did, it seemed like a good idea to get up there and start listening for the voice of the Lord.

I had my real daddy's old Scofield Bible. He used it when he was out preaching the Word and starting churches. In the margin, there were penciled-in notes near verses he had preached on and I started searching through them hoping to find something to get me past my first sermon.

I didn't have a whole lot of luck with that and soon started searching elsewhere to get my message from the Lord. Sunday was approaching and Jerry Stillman and his Little Rock disaster were pressing pretty hard on my mind.

• • •

Sunday morning. Just like that it was Sunday morning. I was three hours away from either being the next Billy Sunday or making a complete jackass out of myself. The odds were the animal kingdom was about to increase faster than the roll of evangelists.

Mama fixed eggs, grits, country salt ham, and red-eye gravy. I may have been fixing to make a fool of myself trying to preach the Word, but if Mama had her way, I was going to do it on a full stomach. In the meantime, Daddy decided to take this time at breakfast to put in his words of wisdom.

"Boy, you got that sermon prepared and ready to lay out for us this morning?"

"Yes, sir."

"What you gonna preach about?"

"I'm preaching on hell, Daddy, and I think I got me a pretty good sermon. Bro. Earl Lee seemed to like it."

Daddy studied me for a minute, "You ain't gonna preach from no notes are you? Lord knows a preacher ain't worth his pay if he has to use something 'sides the Word of the Lord."

"Well," I replied trying to whisper 'cause I knew he was a little hard of hearing, "I do have sort of an outline with a few notes written on it just so I won't forget what I'm gonna say."

Suddenly the good Lord cured his bad hearing and he jumped up from the table knocking his chair over in the commotion. "Don't tell me the Lord has called you to preach and you have to write down something to say. Lord help you, boy. If the Lord called you, you can bet He is gonna tell you what to say. Now where is them notes you got wrote up?"

"I'll get 'em," I said as I went to the living room to get my Bible.

The minute I walked back in the room, he tore into me. He took that Bible and shook all my notes out. Right there in front of me, he tore them up into little pieces. He then ranted and raved about the Lord speaking through me and I didn't need no notes to tell me what to say. In all the years he had been my daddy, I had never seen him act this way. I decided it was best I just keep my mouth shut. Mama seemed to agree.

By the time he got through, I knew three things. First, I knew the Lord hadn't called me to preach. It had been those old men who did the calling. Second, I knew that my well-prepared sermon was laying on the floor in tiny bits of paper. Finally, I knew that this was gonna be the shortest sermon in history. I was in big trouble.

It was time to leave for church so off we went. Mama and Daddy in the front of the truck. My brother, that lowdown slimy scum, and me sitting in the back of the truck with the wind about to blow us out the back of it. Frankly, I was praying for a serious wreck of some sort that would leave me dead. A dead martyr who died on the way to preaching for the Lord. No such luck. We made it safe and sound. When the truck stopped and I looked out, all I could see were cars everywhere. I seriously doubted that the Frostbite Baptist Church had ever had such a gathering.

Well, there ain't no sense in dragging it out. My first sermon was a complete bust. First of all, Bro. Earl Lee took almost 30 minutes to introduce me. By the time he got through, Billy Sunday or St. Paul could not have lived up to that introduction. Then he told folks to settle in because "this here boy is going to be preaching on hell for the next hour or two. So you good folks just settle in and let's spur him on with a few amens along the way."

Then he called on Mr. Harlen Evans to come up and sing "The Ninety and Nine." Mr. Evans made it to the end of the last verse in the neighborhood of five minutes, as it's a very long song when sung in low gear. As I've told you before, Mr. Evans could not carry a tune and the folks present that morning were either crying or stifling a laugh. But either way, they were ready for the boy to now get up and feed their souls from the Word.

For this auspicious occasion my daddy borrowed a wire recorder from one of my uncles over in Jonesboro where the college was located. This was a state-of-the-art recording device that had not been seen in Frostbite. There were two reels. One reel had a thin wire that passed over the recording head and rolled up on the second reel. It was on this wire that my daddy hoped to capture my first sermon for posterity.

Daddy set up the wire recorder under the pulpit and put the microphone right in front of where I would be preaching. He just had to turn it on before I started my sermon. So just as "The Ninety and Nine" was coming to an end and I was ready to step up and launch my career, Daddy came up to turn the recorder on.

So I just stood there while Daddy got under the pulpit to get the thing going. We waited and he worked. Perhaps I ought to mention that my daddy was not electronically inclined. He once electrocuted two of our best hogs because he did not know that if you dropped an electric light into the water trough while they were drinking from it, they would immediately turn into bacon. Said he was just trying to warm up the water for them.

While I stood there feeling very self-conscious, we heard him mumbling, "Damn thing ain't got no juice going to it." Then he raised up and yelled, "R.C., go out there and check the breaker. This thang ain't go no juice going to it."

Then Daddy said to me, "Wait just a minute, boy, and we'll get this thang working. Your mama wants to record this first sermon, so just hold on."

While I was holding on, waiting on this contraption to get working, it suddenly dawned on me that I had to go pee. I don't mean just a minor urge, I am talking about the urge where you hear this little voice in your head that says, "Son, it is time to take care of a little business."

Then I heard Daddy, "Ain't no juice coming to it. R.C., you sure that breaker is on?"

The little voice said, "Son, while they are screwing around with this recorder, you might want to take a little trip out back."

Then a stroke of godly genius came upon me. "Daddy, let me check one spot out back and see if I can fix it." With that I ran from the platform and went back where the Sunday school rooms were and where the restrooms were located. After attending to the needs mentioned by that little voice, I went back to the sanctuary and got back up on the platform.

Really the only thing I had forgotten was that the plumbing in the Frostbite Baptist Church made a noise somewhat similar to a small Niagara Falls. So while I was standing there before the people waiting on Daddy to perform some miracle, the sounds from the flushed toilet were cascading throughout the sanctuary. Mama's face was beet red. Most of the congregation were doubled over laughing. Leroy, my spiritual mentor from the Methodist church, was laying on the floor as tears of laughter flowed down his face.

And then the voice of my daddy, "It's working! Damn thing wasn't turned on. Come on, boy. Lay it on us. I got the recorder working."

There are only a few things in my life that have either been photographed or recorded for posterity, but unfortunately my first sermon is among the esteemed collection. So rather than trying to describe it, I will just give you the exact and painful transcript from the wire recorder that worked perfectly throughout the duration of my entire sermon.

Don't bother to go get a cup of coffee and settle in for a long reading of a spiritual masterpiece. This will only take a minute or two. So here it is, directly from the wire:

Hi, y'all. Today the Lord has laid on my heart that I am suppose' to preach to y'all on hell. My text for today is Matthew 18:9. Let us read it together.

Then I could not find Matthew. My daddy tore up all my notes. Not really being a man of the Word, I did not know where Matthew was to be found. I looked all over the place for that book of the Bible. Then I looked up at the folks in the congregation. Apparently they all found it okay, they were just sitting there, waiting on me.

I had some vague idea that it was in the New Testament, but not the foggiest idea *where* in the New Testament it might be found. Then I remembered the table of contents. Thumbing to the front of my Bible, I did find the table of contents and, sure enough, there was Matthew listed, page 1285. No wonder I couldn't find it. This book was bigger than the Sears catalogue. At least three minutes had passed. I tried to recover.

You will find that verse on page 1285 in your Bible.

I did not take into consideration that not everyone would be using the Scofield King James Version I was using that day — the version, I might add, that was actually written by the men of old, not like some of them feel-good versions that are out there now.

So everyone was confused. Some turned to page 1285. Some were in Matthew, a few were over in Mark, and at least some just closed their Bibles in total confusion. Leroy, once again, had tears running down his stupid Methodist face.

Well there was nothing I could do about getting them all on the same page. I figured that was their problem, so I pressed forward.

Let us read this verse together. Matthew 18, verse nine: "And if your eye causes you to sin, pluck it out and cast it from you. It is better for you to enter into life with one eye, rather than having two eyes, to be cast into hell fire."

Now, this here is my introduction: A lot of people are confused by this verse in the Bible.

What I did not say was that one of the most confused was standing before them. I was missing those notes pretty badly.

Some thank it is about having your eye poked out. But they is wrong. In fact, this don't have nothing to do with eyes. However, eyes are nice to have because we need them to see. I had an uncle one time who was blind and he had a terrible time reading the Bible and stuff like that. But this ain't about being blind. This is about what is worse than being blind. What is worse than being blind is going to hell, which I might add, many in this hell hole called Frostbite, Arkansas, are gonna experience if they don't turn to Jesus.

Bro. Earl Lee said his first "Amen", but I could tell his heart wasn't in it.

Now I got three points to this sermon. Let me tell you what my first point is. Here it is.

Point #1
Life without God is a hell of a way to live.

I think this point speaks for itself. What more can I say than "Life without God is a hell of a way to live." I mean, if you don't get that point real clear then there ain't a lot I can say for you. You know what I mean!

It's just like old Noah and the whale. He got in that whale and was away from God and inside that whale old Noah felt like hell. Y'all know what I mean?

Right about that time, several things were going on. Mama's face was real red, and I could tell she was struggling right along with me. Thank you, Lord, for Mama. Daddy had his head down. If the truth were known, he was praying that the recorder wasn't working. Leroy, bless his filthy Methodist soul, had his face all crunched up trying to keep from busting out laughing. And I was feeling less called by the minute. Also, I was out of material for point number one. That was all I could remember from the three pages of notes that were lying on our kitchen floor. In the back of my mind, for some reason, Noah and the whale just didn't seem right. Wished I had them notes.

Now let me move on to point #2.
Life without God is a hell of a way to die.

Now what the Lord is trying to tell us in this point is that we are going to die and if we die without Him, we are going to hell.

I heard a slight "Amen, preach on" come from the lips of Bro. Earl Lee. But again, you could tell his heart wasn't really in it. Leroy had a temporary coughing fit and I hoped he would die and find out about hell. Mama was starting to grin. Daddy was working hard to kill power to the recorder. Things were moving right along.

Which leads me to my third and final point.
Life without God is a hell of a way to spend eternity.

If you die and you go to hell, you are going to spend your whole life there and it is gonna be hot and you are going to miss your mama's cooking and it is going to be hell.

So that is my sermon for you today. Let's stand and sing "Just As I Am Without One Plea." And if you want to come to Jesus today, come on up here and talk to Bro. Earl Lee because he knows about that stuff and I don't yet.

Let us stand.

Now all I had left to say was "Thank the Lord for Miss Elle" because the piano was so loud that the congregation could not hear that sorry Leroy as he doubled over in pain laughing at my predicament.

We sang one quick verse. Since no one rushed up the aisle to confess their sins and stay out of hell, I assumed I had done a pretty lousy job. The only good thing about my sermon was that it only lasted about five minutes, including dramatic pauses, and because of that, we would even beat the Methodists — although most of them were sitting right there in front of me — to the BBQ joint.

What I forgot was that Bro. Earl Lee probably had a few words. He did. Daddy caught them on the same wire he recorded my sermon on. As he said later, there was plenty of time left so he didn't need to change nothing to get Bro. Earl Lee's words too.

From the tape these are the exact words Bro. Earl Lee spoke:

Well, well, well. Now wasn't that a nice little sermonette? I think the boy had the right notion, he just got it over pretty quick. Seems like what he meant to say was something like this.

And for the next one hour and 15 minutes, he cut loose on my three points and he preached like the devil was at the door just waiting to drag us all into hell. He raved and he ranted. Sweat broke out all over his face and he took his coat off and flung it over the choir rail and cut loose some more. It was a sight to see.

And when he finally ran down and his voice was hoarse from exhaustion, he just sort of paused and said, "Now that's what I think the boy was trying to tell us."

He said a closing prayer. As he walked off the podium, he just sort of leaned over to me and said, "Boy, looks like me and you got some work to do."

Somehow I think Bro. Earl Lee and the elders were trying to figure out how to recall the call, but once you laid it on about God telling you that I was supposed to be in the ministry, there was just not much taking back that could be done.

I don't remember much about the rest of that day. We went home and things at the dinner table were real quiet. I do remember hearing Daddy say to Mama, "Yea, I got it all right. Every word of it. You might know the damn recorder would work."

Eight

As I was figuring that being a preacher wasn't as easy as I thought it looked, I decided to put in some serious study on the project. It seemed to me that Leroy, that sorry, no-good Methodist heathen, was not going to be the fine source of Biblical training that I needed. Obviously, Bro. Earl Lee lost a little confidence in his protégé and was not going to be spending a lot of time with my personal development. So as far as I could tell, it was going to take a little self-help study to move me along the way.

My first step was to take an objective look at my first sermon. After some minutes of analysis, I came to the conclusion that the main problem with it was that it just stunk. For the next week, more folks were talking about the wire recorder and the flushing toilet than escaping from hell. Folks seemed to miss the point.

It also occurred to me that maybe I relied on those notes a little too much. Once my daddy had shredded them, I was pretty much out of material. So, with some hesitation that my friends might find out where I was going for information, I decided to get the Bible down and see what it had to say. This was a new approach for me, but I was sort of desperate.

Several things impressed me about this first personal encounter with the Bible. First, it was big. I mean, who would ever have time to read something that big? As best I can remember, my longest book up to that time was *Tom*

Sawyer and it seemed to me that the Bible was about 10 times bigger than that fine story. So my first move was to cut that Bible down to preaching size. Right off the bat, I dropped off the Old Testament since as far as I could tell, all the good stuff was in the New Testament anyway.

The second thing that impressed me was that there seemed to be a lot of verses that were a little tedious. I tried working through all those "begot" verses right there near the front of the New Testament and decided they had to go. Pretty soon I was going to have this down to reading size.

Finally, I was impressed by the fact that no matter how much I cut out, I didn't know anything about what was left. Things were not looking promising for this future Biblical scholar. In fact, going it on my own was looking pretty risky. I decided to go see Bro. Webb down at the Methodist church. He was the most educated preacher in town and seemed to take a pretty practical view of preaching anyway. He wasn't as fired up as Bro. Earl Lee, but he usually made more sense.

•••

On the Monday after my preaching fiasco, I was walking to my grandma's house after school and saw Bro. Webb's old car in front of the Methodist church. Since he had what he called an "open door policy" at his church, meaning that anyone was free to just open his door and walk in, I did just that.

Bro. Webb had the *Blytheville Courier News,* all eight pages of the nearest daily newspaper around, spread out on his desk and he was working the crossword puzzle. In front of him sat a half-eaten spam and tomato sandwich with mayo oozing over the bread crust.

He didn't look up, "What's a five-letter word meaning 'on balance'?"

Figuring he was talking to me I thought a minute and said, "Sounds like 'level' to me."

"Damn, boy. I think you got one. I been studying them five spaces for 10 minutes, but I think you're right on. Let's see."

He paused looking back over his afternoon's work, "Yea, 14 down is 'lover' so that starts with L just like ... damn right, you got it boy. 'Preciate it. So what can I do for you?"

"Bro. Webb, how come you say damn and hell so much? Bro. Earl Lee would write me off to the devil if he heard me say those words."

"Boy, your daddy says hell and damn every now and again, don't he? Well, I learned a long time ago that a little lay participation was good for the preacher in that it helped the people relate to him. Now let me ask you this. If your daddy was going squirrel huntin', who'd you think he would rather be around, me or Earl Lee?"

About that time I figured Daddy wouldn't be too high on either one 'cause Bro. Earl Lee couldn't keep his mouth shut and Bro. Webb would lumber through the woods like a WWII Sherman tank, but I did get Bro. Webb's point.

"I reckon he would rather have you, Bro. Webb 'cause you're more like him than Bro. Earl Lee."

"Damn right I am. When you go off preaching, don't get so uppity you can't lay a little hell or damn on them from time to time." He bit off a bite of that spam sandwich. With a mouth full of food he said, "But 'at ain't why you here so what's on your mind, boy?"

I'm telling you I about threw up every time I saw that man eat. But anyway, I kept plugging along, "I just wanted to talk to you 'bout that sermon I preached last Sunday. Guess you heard about it, seems like everybody else did."

He chuckled a little, took a big drink of his iced tea, and stared right at me. "Son, I heard it was a little short and about as deep as a tadpole hole, but seems like you done all right for your first go around. I was planning on hearing you, but by the time I got there Earl Lee was giving his two-hour summation of what you said, so I just passed on by. I still heard you done pretty good."

"Well, I don't know about that, but I was wondering if you had some books or something I could read so I could lay some pretty stout stuff on them next time. You know what I mean?"

Bro. Webb got up from his desk, wiped his mouth on his sleeve, and walked over to a big bookcase on the wall across from the window. It was just packed full of books, and I could not imagine what he was going to give me. Finally after looking things over for a long time, he reached up and pulled down an old Bible just like the one we had at home. He studied it for a minute and then handed it to me.

"Son, you ever hear of Billy Sunday?"

"Well I guess I sure have. He was about the biggest preacher ever come down the pike. I hear tell he preached one time at the football field in Jonesboro and the whole town came out. You bet I know who that man was."

Bro. Webb went on, "Well, I knew him first-hand. I heard him say one time that, after he got saved and started preaching, he just felt the hand of God on him. That went on for a while and Billy decided he needed to get away from just preaching the Gospel and start laying a little philosophy on the people.

"He said that no sooner than he done that, the Spirit left him and he dried up inside like an old man. Said it was the worst thing that ever happened to him."

I got a little confused 'cause I didn't really know what philosophy was so I decided to get Bro. Webb back to the subject. "That's good," I said, "but I don't see what that's got to do with what I'm asking about."

Bro. Webb explained, "Son, look at that Bible I just put in your hand. Go home and read it and don't try to complicate it up none. The message of God is simple, easy to understand, and elementary in implementation. You just worry about preaching from the Bible and let God worry about making it fit the people in the pew. You know what I mean?

"Now get on out of here and start getting ready for another sermon. You know Earl Lee's gonna have you preaching again soon as he gets over the shock of your last one. Bless you, boy. Now git."

Nine

After leaving the Methodist church, I went home to hide out for the rest of the day. Unfortunately, Mama had made a list of things she needed from the store. She found me out under the willow tree in front of the house and, before I knew what was happening, she sent me back to town to pick them up from Mr. R.C.'s store.

I dreaded going through town with a passion. By now everyone knew I preached the shortest sermon in the history of preaching in the Frostbite Baptist Church. There might have been someone who came in under five minutes, but if so, he was not known in our parts.

Bro. Earl Lee was my biggest worry, with Leroy right behind him. Bro. Earl Lee worried me because I knew I disappointed him. Leroy worried me because I knew he pulled one over on me by giving me one of those sorry sermonette outlines they preached down at the Methodist church.

Those two were my main worries, but the other 170 residents of town were not on my "can't wait to see" list either, if you know what I mean. There is just something unpleasant about running into a bunch of people who are laughing about the sideshow down at the Frostbite Baptist Church the previous Sunday, especially when you were the show.

I planned my strategy well. Since we lived about two miles from town and my only means of transportation was the pair of feet the good Lord gave me, I could approach town from any direction I found suitable. Mr. R.C's store was on the exact opposite side of town from where we lived. So not wanting to cross all four streets of the town and not wanting to run into anyone I knew, I decided on a rear attack.

My plan was simple. Right after I crossed Morgan's Creek, I would head north across Mr. Ledbetter's cotton field. Then about a quarter of a mile north of town, I would start to circle back behind the high school, through the back yard of old Miss Johnson's house, and then along the wall of the First Baptist Church building. From behind that church building where the black folks had spent all day Sunday preaching and praising while I was sermonetting and whimpering, I could run about 50 feet and be at Mr. R.C.'s store.

I mounted my approach. All was fine until Mr. Ledbetter drove up to look at his crop about the time I was entering his field. Mr. Ledbetter was not one to excuse trespassing. That big Cadillac slid to a stop just as I was crossing the ditch to move across his field.

That man was on me in no time flat. "Hey, boy! What the hell you doing goin' into my field to trample down my cotton? Answer me, boy."

I answered quickly, "It's just me, Mr. Ledbetter. I'm just Elroy and Martha's boy, and I didn't mean no harm to your cotton. Just sort of rounding the corner to get to Mr. R.C.'s store."

"Good Lord, boy, I didn't know it was you. Can't see as well as I used to could. You that boy who done preached over at the Baptist church yesterday, ain't you?"

Well, what could I say? He was either talking about me or Bro. Earl Lee, and I don't think he was referring to Bro. Earl Lee. "Yes, sir, that was me. I preached my first sermon, such as it was."

"How much did Earl Lee pay you to preach that sermon, boy?"

"Weren't no pay in it, Mr. Ledbetter. I think he asked me to preach to give me some experience. I pretty much think the whole town would agree that I needed the experience. You hear much about that sermon of mine?"

I could tell he was about to get a little laugh started, but he tried to hold it back. "Yea, I heard 'bout that sermon, such as it was. I hear you had 'em going to hell, and you got them there in under five minutes. Get in the car, boy. I'm gonna drive you over to R.C.'s store."

So much for my stealth approach. What could I do but get in the car and try to slink down so no one would see me. Mr. Ledbetter never drove more than five miles an hour and I figured, at best, this was going to be a 10-minute trip. He made a few turns and then stopped. I looked out and we had stopped right in the middle of town at the post office. In Frostbite, Arkansas, the post office was second only to church for getting up a crowd. And to my dismay, the morning crowd was still there. Nancy Fay Stillman was the first one to spot me in Mr. Ledbetter's big car. Nancy Fay was Jerry's sister, but she didn't have a sports car like Jerry.

She ran over and motioned for me to roll down the window. Hardly before I could get the window down, she had her arm around me giving me a big hug and a kiss. Lord, I like to of died. What was this crazy girl doing? Nancy Fay was a senior in high school, a cheerleader, and as good looking as Mama's fried chicken on the Sunday table.

Before I could take it all in, she was all over me again, "Lordy, Lordy, Sam Hamilton I am so proud of you. Yesterday up there in that pulpit I swear I just heard the voice of God as you preached from the Holy Word. Fact is, I went home and told my mama that I could just about marry someone with the gift the Lord had placed on you. Lordy, Lordy, you was something up there in that fine suit of yours."

Before she could grab me again, Mr. Ledbetter was back in the car and pulling away from the post office at his top speed of 10 miles per hour. No tires were spinning. "Boy, looks like you got you a woman, don't it? That Stillman girl was all over you. Of course, you got to get used to that if you gonna preach the Word. Preachers are lot like Elvis and them other big stars. Women can't keep they hands off them."

I knew old man Ledbetter was as crazy as a loon, but about that moment I thought I might rethink this preaching stuff. Maybe those five old men knew what they were talking about.

"Mr. Ledbetter, can I ask you a question?"

"Go on, boy. I figure I know what you gonna ask, but go on anyway."

"Well, I was just wonderin' if you was a Christian?" My mama said old man Ledbetter, whose wife of 34 years died about 10 years ago and who in the meantime built somewhat of a reputation with the women around the county, would date a goat if he got a chance. But with him comparing me to Elvis and all, I was sort of starting to like the old man. At least I figured he knew something about the social requirements facing me.

"What you think?" he said with a kind of snarl on his face.

"My daddy says you're a good man, but don't turn my back on you in a poker game 'cause you would have five aces before the next hand was dealt. But I don't know whether you ever gave your everlasting soul to Jesus and stuff like that."

Right about then he started getting pretty red in the face, and I could see I was on some shaky ground. But it was too late. I had already asked.

"Let me tell you something, boy. A man like me ain't got no use for that Jesus stuff. I worked hard for every dime I got and the Lord ain't had nothing to do with it. I ain't saying you ought not be no preacher if that's what you think is right, but don't be trying none of that gettin' saved stuff on me."

About that time we pulled up to Mr. R.C.'s store and Mr. Ledbetter just sort of stared ahead with both hands on the steering wheel of that big Cadillac. I could tell I upset him so I just said something like "thank you for the ride" and got out and slammed the door. I hadn't been a preacher but 24 hours and had already preached a lousy sermon and made the richest man in the county madder than hell. I was off to some start.

•••

Mr. R.C.'s store was the only grocery store in town. Everybody from miles around had an account there. They would charge things all year long and then, when the crop came in, they would pay Mr. R.C. off just like they did the gin and the bank. Every family had their own individual paper pad, and all those pads hung in a rack by the cash register. Usually you would just go in and pick up something your mama sent you to buy and as you walked out of the store, you would hold it up for Mr. R.C. to see. Then he would write it down on your family's charge pad and your daddy would pay for it when the crop came in later that year.

I remember being in there when one of the Longfellow girls came in to buy something. I don't remember her name, but she was just about knee high and Mr. R.C. didn't know who she belonged to either.

My friend, Charley Hudson, and I were in there having a root beer and a moon pie when this little old girl came in and went straight over and picked up a roll of toilet tissue. As she started to walk out, she just held it up and walked on. Since Mr. R.C. didn't know whose kid she was, he yelled out, "Wait a minute, little darling. Who's that for?"

Yelling back as she slammed the door, she said, "We all gonna use it, Mr. R.C.!" I thought old Hud and I would burst out laughing we were so tickled. Even Mr. R.C. kind of had a grin on his face. He just looked at us and said, "Well, they may all be gonna use it but looks like I'm gonna pay for it." Mr. R.C. was like that. He was just a funny, nice grocery man. That's why we all liked to hang around his store. There was always something going on like that.

But on this day, Mama had sent me after some Arm and Hammer baking soda and some Epsom salts. I hoped she didn't get them mixed up. Bless her heart, my mama may have been the worst cook in Arkansas. One Christmas she made something called "heavenly hash," which was supposed to be made out of coconut and marshmallows and good stuff like that. Probably would have been real good, but Mama got the coconut mixed up with a bar of Ivory soap and grated soap into the recipe. We foamed at the mouth till way past New Year's Eve.

Anyway, I got the stuff Mama needed and showed it to Mr. R.C. so he could put it on the book for us. Sometimes, when he was real busy, folks would try to get out without holding their stuff up for him to see. Mama said she would kill me if I even thought about doing something like that so I always made sure he saw what I had in my hand. Not that I would have tried to sneak out without paying anyway. I mean if you're gonna be a preacher, you might go for the "ministerial discount" I was later to learn about, but you wouldn't steal anything on purpose.

Just as I got out the door I saw Moses coming over to the store to go to work. You may remember that during the week he worked for Mr. R.C. sacking groceries and carrying bags to the cars and such, but on Sunday he was the pastor over at the First Baptist Church. The one and only black church in Frostbite, Arkansas.

Soon as he saw me he called out, "Bro. Sam, you got a minute I could talk to you?"

Man, I didn't know what to think. That black man had called me "brother." I didn't know whether I was to call him Mr. Moses, as my mama had taught me, or Rev. Moses like he was on Sunday. So I just walked over where he was and we started talking like we always did.

"Mr. Moses, how come you called me Brother Sam? You just always called me 'boy' like everyone else. How come today you called me 'brother'?"

"I did that because we is now brothers in the Lord. I may be blacker than mud and you may be whiter than a new-washed sheet, but now that the Lord has laid His hand on you, we is now brothers. So I'm being respectful of your call just like folks are to me on Sunday when they call me Rev. Moses. You see how it works?"

I figured I did, but I also knew that it wasn't going set too well with folks around town to have a black man calling me Bro. Sam. I decided to just agree that we were brothers in the Lord and let it go at that.

"Heard you did a pretty good job preaching yeste'day at the white church." Black folks hardly ever called it the Frostbite Baptist Church because of the feud over being first and all.

"Well, I guess you heard wrong. I was gonna preach on hell and before I could get the fire burning I ran out of anything to say. I wouldn't say I did a pretty good job."

He kind of grinned and I think he even winked at me, "Well, I did hear it was kind of short. But folks say you done real good. How come you think you ran out of something to say so fast?"

I told him about my daddy tearing up my notes where I had written down what I was going to say, and how trying to make it up as I went along just didn't seem to work.

He shook his head and got real serious like. "Bro. Sam, you know I'm a lot older than you and I been preaching for a long time. Now Bro. Earl Lee, God bless his old sinful heart, ain't never gonna teach you how to preach 'cause he can't stand the competition. You ever tell anyone I said that and you know what they gonna do to me, but you know it's true.

"So, I don't want to be out of place or nothing, but if you was of mind to let me, I'd be glad to give you a little preaching teaching on the side. What you think about that?"

What did I think about that! I still shook in my shoes ever time I remembered that sermon he preached about the church naming. That man could raise the roof and talk straight to God if he wanted to.

I got so excited I forgot to Bro. or Mr. him, "Lord, Moses, if you could teach me to preach like you I might just like it in this preaching game. Lordy, Lordy, Lordy. I can't believe you would teach me how to preach. You just tell me when you want to get started and I'll be there."

He thought for a minute and then said in kind of a whispery voice, "Well, you know you can't come over to no black church to meet me. And I ain't about to go to no white church to meet with you, so how about we meet on this here bench every morning about 9 o'clock? I don't go to work till 10, and you don't start school for another month or so. We could get in some preaching lessons out here while folks just think we be talking."

"Wow, Mr. Moses," I said now that I got my manners back, "when you want to start?"

"We'll it ain't but quarter-after right now, so what about a little lesson while we here?"

"Sounds good to me. What you think I ought to know?"

You could tell he had already thought it through because he just jumped right in. "Well, Bro. Sam, the starting place in preaching ain't got nothing to do with preaching. It's got to do with what you believe in your heart about the Lord Jesus Christ. Now I wants to hear about you getting saved and all 'cause if that ain't right, then ain't nothing we gonna do gonna make you a preacher."

Thank the Lord I didn't have any trouble with that part. I told Mr. Moses about how when I was 11 years old, Bro. Earl Lee had preached on accepting Jesus as your Lord and Savior and how I had decided to do just that. I told Mr. Moses about how I went up at the altar call and asked the Lord to forgive me of my sins, and how it felt good all over, and how my mama was praising the Lord all the time I was up there on my knees. I told him about going home that day and how Mama and Daddy took time after lunch to talk to me about what it really meant to be a Christian, and how they wanted me to know this was an important decision that could only be made by me.

Then I told Mr. Moses about talking again with Bro. Earl Lee, and how Bro. Earl Lee had told me that it was up to me. I couldn't be doing it just because Bubba and Sara Jane had done it the week before. After everyone was satisfied I knew what I was doing, then I was baptized in the dunking way just like Jesus. I told Mr. Moses how I felt saved from my head to my toes. And all the time I was telling Mr. Moses, he was saying things like "yes, thank you, Lord, that's sure it" and "thank you, Jesus, the boy has got it" and "ain't no doubt — yes, thank you, Jesus." He was thanking Jesus so much it was hard to concentrate on my story.

Finally Mr. Moses said, "You sure got it. Ain't no doubt in my mind. The Lord done saved you from the devil's clutches. Thank you, Jesus. Once you got that down, then you got something to preach about. But right now, I got to go work for Mr. R.C. We gonna meet here in the morning?"

"I'll sure be here, Mr. Moses. What we gonna talk about tomorrow?"

"Well now, tomorrow how's about you talk to me about how the Lord done called you to preach His holy Word. You be thinking about that and I want to hear all about it."

And with that, Mr. Moses got up and went in the store to go to work and I went into my first real case of holy depression. I knew my saving story was as true as the Bible and that my calling story didn't have nothing to do with the Lord. I took Mama's baking soda and Epsom salts home, then I went for a long walk down by Morgan's Creek. I had to come up with something fast if I was going to have something for Mr. Moses the next day.

• • •

Sure enough at straight up 9 o'clock the next morning, Mr. Moses was sitting on the bench in front of Mr. R.C.'s store. When I got there he jumped right in, just like I knew he would. This man was some kind of serious about teaching me the preaching business.

"What you got to say about the Lord calling you into the preaching business?" I mean just like that. No "hello, how are you?" or nothing. He just jumped right in.

"Mr. Moses," I said sort of reluctant-like, "I don't know much about the calling business. I just know Bro. Earl Lee and four elders of the church came over to my house and told me the Lord had laid a call on me."

"You didn't hear the voice of the Lord like Moses or Paul in the Bible did?"

Well, I have to tell you, I didn't know Moses in the Bible had ever heard a call and I didn't know who Paul was so I just told Mr. Moses that I didn't believe I had ever had a call actually in the voice of the Lord Himself.

Mr. Moses thought for a minute, then explained, "I don't have no doubt white folks do it different so maybe that elder stuff is the way you get called. Don't make no sense to me, but let's just go on 'cause if the Lord ain't called you, you gonna know it soon enough.

"I believe I can help you most by just telling you about preaching. I heard Bro. Earl Lee preach a few times and the man has got the blessin' on him, but he ain't got no rhythm in his soul. Folks like to feel a little stirrin' when they are hearing the Word. You don't have to have no long sermon, but you got to have the rhythm. You know what I mean?"

"Mr. Moses, all's I know is that when you preached down at our church on that naming situation, there was some powerful rhythm in that church that day. My mama said she ain't felt that good in her spiritual soul since the last time the Spirit moved her when she was just a girl. I don't know what you did, but it did have some powerful rhythm."

He smiled like he was happy I liked his sermon and then he got right back to the subject. "Well, if you got the rhythm, you don't need a lot of words. The Lord gonna supply the words in the people's hearts, but you just got to keep the rhythm up.

"There are four things you got to get down. You got to be able to say, 'Thank you, Jesus. Say Amen.' That's the first. Now you say it."

"Thank you, Jesus. Say Amen!"

"Yea, well we got some work to do, I can see that right off. Now the second one you got to get down is 'Put your hands up and clap for Jesus.' I ain't gonna ask you to say that because you ain't close to being able to get that one right.

"Then there is the third one you got to get down, 'Am I preaching the truth or ain't I?' Now that one you can work in with the first one. It sounds like this. 'Am I preaching the truth or ain't I?' then you throw in a connector like 'You know I is!' then use that first one, 'Thank you, Jesus. Say Amen!' Now you try to put all that together."

I tell you I didn't want to mess that one up. I thought about it a long time then I said, "Is I preaching the truth or ain't I? You know I is! So thank you, Jesus, and say Amen!"

Mr. Moses just beamed he had such a big smile on his face. "Bro. Sam, there may be hope for you yet. You work on them sayings and we gonna get together tomorrow."

"But, Mr. Moses, you said there were four sayings. What is the fourth?"

"Oh, Lord, I was about to forget the main one. Now listen real close 'cause you want to get this one right. You just bow your head and say, 'Now let us stand and bring offerings unto the Lord.'"

Then he laid back his head and laughed at the top of his voice. "Yes, sir, Bro. Sam. You get that one down 'cause you gonna do some good with that one. I'll see you in the morning, Bro. Sam. Don't worry none 'cause you doing real good."

I left feeling pretty good about the way things were moving, but I didn't go to preaching school the next day. In fact, a couple of weeks would pass before I could sit with Bro. Moses on the bench again.

Daddy said the summer wheat was ready to thrash. We all got up early the next day and took the combine to the field. Daddy drove the tractor to pull the combine, Mama stood on the combine to tie the sacks as they filled up, and I tossed the filled sacks on a trailer to take to the broker. It was hard, back-breaking work. It lasted for a couple of weeks.

So during that time, I had to miss my preaching lessons with Mr. Moses, but I did practice my rhythm and my phrases. I would get in front of the mirror late at night and hold my Bible and lay a few "Thank you, Jesus. Say Amen!" phrases on my image. Then just for fun, I would do that one about the offerings. By the time I was free to visit with Mr. Moses again, he was as eager to hear my preaching phrases as I was to lay them on him.

When I got through saying them all for him, that man actually had tears in his eyes. "Bro. Sam, you is coming right along. We gonna make it yet."

For the next few weeks we worked almost every day. He taught me how to drag a Scripture out and make it last. He taught me how to add a few words and how to throw in a few of those phrases he had taught me.

You take that verse about Jesus going up into the mountain. Now in a white service the preacher might just say, "Jesus went up into the mountain." But in a black service, the way Mr. Moses was teaching me, you could make those six words last a long time. It might go like this:

Now the Word of the Lord says that Jesus went up into the mountain. Say Amen. Now I ask you "where" did the Lord go? He went up into the mountain. He didn't mess with no hills. No sir, when the Lord does something, He does it in a big way, so I ask you again, "where" did He go? He went up into the mountain. Thank you, Jesus. Say Amen!

Now the Word says "who" went up into the mountain. Who was it? Well, it was Jesus. He didn't send no second lieutenant. He didn't send no first sergeant. He didn't send no private first class. No sir, when the job in the mountain was to be done, Jesus sent His own self. Say Amen! and give Jesus a hand.

Now Jesus did "what"? Jesus went somewhere. He could have been sitting home reading the paper. He could have been taking a nap. But what did Jesus do? That man went somewhere. Now give Jesus a hand and say Amen! 'Cause that's what we need to do. We need to go somewhere. Where do we need to go? We need to go to the mountain.

Enough people staying in the valley. Enough people sittin' around. But Jesus got up and went to the mountain, ain't I telling you? Say Amen! and give Jesus a hand for getting up and going to the mountain.

That man could get more out of six words than I could ever dream of finding. But he was teaching me that you can take a few words and make a long sermon out of them if you got the rhythm and the phrases to make the words live.

Weeks passed and, day after day, Mr. Moses taught me how to preach the Word. He taught me how to make an altar call to bring people to Jesus. He gave me hints on how to "lift the offering" and some of the other more important aspects of the service. It was better than any seminary class I would ever attend and would serve me well for years to come.

But the fact was that what I was learning, I wasn't asked to use anywhere. When I asked Bro. Earl Lee when I would be preaching again, he just said, "In the Lord's own time, boy. In the Lord's own time." I didn't know what that meant, but I did know it had been over a month since my first five-minute sermon and it just seemed like if the Lord had called me, He ought to be giving me somewhere to preach.

What I think happened was word got out about how bad I was. Not many preachers wanted to invite some five-minute wonder into their church and know they were going to have to apologize to the people for having invited him. Whatever the cause, my invitations to preach were limited.

One Thursday morning I was back on the bench with Mr. Moses. I guess all told we had been on that bench at least 10 to 15 times, and every time I learned something new on loving the Lord or preaching the Word. I had come to look forward to being with him. In our town, it wasn't uncommon for blacks and whites to be friends so no one questioned the time I spent with him. Those were wonderful days.

But on this particular morning, the late August heat bore down on us even at 9 o'clock. I was the first to speak, "Bro. Moses, what you think we need to work on today?"

He thought for a minute. Then he leaned over and put his head in his hands. I had seen him do that before. It always meant he was thinking real hard about what to say. My heart stopped. Maybe I had flunked out of the preaching class. I can't say for sure, but it seemed like 10 minutes passed before he spoke.

"Bro. Sam, I think you is ready. I done taught you all I know, and you seem to have learned it pretty good. I been praying about this and I know we could both get in trouble, but what about you preaching at our church Sunday morning after next? We got a visiting preacher coming from Memphis this Sunday, but the Sunday after this one, I would like for you to preach for us. That would give us a couple of weeks to work on your sermon. I do believe you are ready.

"Now before you say you will, you got to remember this here is Arkansas and some folks don't take kindly to white folks mixing with black folks. You could be settin' your preaching back a long time it you do this, but I sure would like to have you preach to us, if you would."

I couldn't breath. Someone *wanted* me to preach. Someone wanted *me* to preach. Someone wanted me to *preach?* I didn't care if the congregation was black or red or purple, I was ready to go. I had enough preaching backed up in me that I thought I would explode.

I could not wait to tell Bro. Earl Lee that the Lord had opened up a place for me to preach the Holy Word.

•••

"You gonna what?!"

Bro. Earl Lee was fit to be killed, "Lord, boy, what do you mean you gonna preach down at the nigger church? You ain't even got to going good in the white church much less to be messing around down there. Boy, it just ain't right."

I figured that was one of those times where anything I said was going to be wrong so I just let him have at me. He told me that the whole town would turn against me, no church would ever ask me to preach again, and that the good Lord Himself would not smile upon a white boy starting out his preaching career down at no nigger church.

Finally I figured I was gonna have to say something so I jumped in, "Well, Bro. Earl Lee, looks to me like if I'm ever gonna get to preach again, it's gonna have to be down at the black church because I ain't been overwhelmed with invitations to come to no white church and preach."

I had him! It had been months since that first sermon and not once had anyone called on me to pray, much less preach. I knew for a fact that Bro. Settlemire over at the Gosnel Baptist Church, a church started by my real daddy

I might add, asked Bro. Earl Lee about me coming over there to preach and Bro. Earl Lee was quite generous in his rejecting of the idea.

I had him in a corner, but he decided to counterattack. "Boy, this here's what we gonna do. You tell Moses you can't preach over there because on that very Sunday morning, you gonna be preaching for me. Now you go tell him that. Right now."

"Bro. Earl Lee, I can't do that. He asked me to preach for him and I'm gonna keep my word. They may all be black as dirt, but they want me to preach for them and I'm gonna do it." I didn't tell him Mr. Moses had been training me. Lord knows I didn't want to hear the storm that would stir up!

Then his tone changed, "What's your mama think about this little preaching engagement you done gone ahead and scheduled?"

"I ain't told her yet. You are the first one to know 'cause I thought you would be proud I had a place to preach."

"Well, let's just see what she has to say about it, mister. I got me a feeling you and the niggers ain't gonna be doing much singing and shoutin' together in the near future. Now get on out of here and let me know what she has to say about this little idea of yours." And he sent me on my way.

For the first time in my life, Bro. Earl Lee called me "mister." I assumed he had given me a promotion from "boy" and that the promotion was good.

On the other hand, he had me scared to go home and tell Mama what I had agreed to do. So feeling proud of the promotion on the one hand and scared out of my wits on the other, I headed home trying to figure out how to break the news of my scheduled preaching engagement to Mama.

Ten

FROSTBITE, ARKANSAS, DID NOT have a newspaper. Frostbite, Arkansas, did not have a radio station. What Frostbite, Arkansas, did have was an official United States post office where all news sources reported in every 15 minutes to make certain anyone going to get their mail would be informed up to the minute.

Now, unknown to me, during the time Bro. Earl Lee was giving me his spiritual counsel, Mama had been visiting at the post office. I do not know the exact timing of the news release that I had accepted an invitation to preach at the all-black First Baptist Church, nor do I know the source of the news report, but Mama had the full story long before I walked back across Morgan's Creek and headed for home. Mama told Daddy. My brother, Danny, heard Mama tell Daddy. So in all, I had a pretty informed audience waiting for me when I walked in the house.

Mama spoke first, "I hear you gonna be preaching down at the black folks' church next week. That true?"

I told her it was and then braced myself for whatever was to come. No one said anything. I finally looked up and saw tears in her eyes. Daddy was just looking down at his boots. My brother, the lazy, good-for-nothing SOB, was grinning from ear to ear.

Finally, Mama got her composure. "Well, son, I think you have done stirred up a hornet's nest, but I'm proud of you. I'm gonna be praying for you. Me and your Daddy will be right there on the front row to support you in your preaching."

"Damn right!" Daddy was pretty much a man of few words.

My brother just grinned, that sorry devil.

I felt the need to say something. "Bro. Earl Lee don't want me to do it. Says won't no white church will ever let me preach for them again. But I feel it's the right thing to do. I really think the Lord wants me to do it." If you really didn't have a good case for doing something, it always helped to throw in that "the Lord wants me to do it." Who could argue with that?

Daddy got up from his chair and walked over to where his cap was hanging. He took it off the peg and rolled it around in his hands for a minute without saying anything or even looking up. Then he just walked over and put his hand on my shoulder and in a real low voice said, "Boy, you done right. You gonna take some grief for it, but you done right and don't you let Earl Lee or anyone else tell you different. Any of them gets on you too hard, you let me know and I'll beat the holy hell out of them." Then having given me his full support he just turned and walked out the door.

"Guess, I better start supper," Mama said as she left the room.

Now it is just me and my brother, good old Danny boy. I knew what was coming, least I had a good idea. "Gonna preach for the niggers, are you? You sorry bastard, you gonna get us both killed." Then he left the room.

So at least I knew where everybody in the family stood on the news. A time for prayer:

Dear Lord, I done jumped in the creek. At least teach me how to swim. I pray you won't let nobody take nothing out on Rev. Moses. He is just trying to help and don't need no grief from it. Also, Lord, if you don't mind, I would appreciate it if you don't let me make a fool out of myself and a laughing stock out of my family. And Lord, don't let my brother be right. I ain't one for being killed before I get started. Amen.

•••

The days passed faster than a north wind and every day brought a new development.

Bro. Earl Lee got up the following Sunday and told everybody in attendance at the Frostbite Baptist Church that I was going "down the road to preach at the nigger church" the following Sunday. He said, "Just thought y'all might want to know!"

All week long, every time I would pass someone in the hall at school, I would hear them whisper something. I usually couldn't understand it, but I had an idea what was said.

On the Wednesday before I was to preach the next Sunday, one of the boys in the senior class decided to make an example out of me at the lunch break. His name was Tommy Joe Hillard, called T.J. by most of us, and he was the oldest and the biggest of nine brothers.

While T.J. was a senior, he was also 21 years old, weighed about 250, and stood about a foot taller than me. He was a little slow, had spent two years in the first, fourth and eight grades, and obviously had developed some strong racial feelings down through the years.

Everyone knew I was in trouble when he sat down by Leroy and me in the lunch room. Including me. About six of his buddies were sittin' about three tables over ready for the show. I figured I might as well get it started, the sooner it'd be over with.

"How you doing, T.J.?"

"Hear you gonna do a little nigger preaching this Sunday. What I hear right?"

"Yea, I need a little practice so I'm gonna lay a little on them," I replied trying to kind of make it sound like no big thing.

"Well, well. If you like them niggers so much, you must know how to shine shoes pretty good. How about you just get down under the table and do a little shinin' on mine?"

"Oh, T.J., don't start nothing. This ain't got ..."

I didn't even get to finish the sentence. Before I knew it, he had that big hand of his around my neck and had started pushing my face under the table. "Lick them shoes, nigger lover, make 'em shine."

About that time, I felt his hand release. Things got real quiet and I heard this strange voice say, "T.J., turn him loose or I'm gonna cut your throat from ear to ear." I felt the hand relax even more. When I looked up, there was Danny — my brother? — with his pocketknife stuck right up under T.J.'s neck.

Danny told T.J., "Now, tell him you are sorry and that you gonna be praying he does a real good job next Sunday." Frankly, I thought Danny was pushing our luck, but then I heard T.J. promising sincere prayer support for my forthcoming service.

About that time I saw Mrs. Crocker, our math teacher, coming over. "Anything wrong over here, boys?"

"No, ma'am. T.J. was just having a little word of prayer for my little brother as he prepares to preach the Word next Sunday. That's all, ain't it, T.J.?"

T.J. mumbled his undying support for me, and Mrs. Crocker sort of grinned and walked away. Then I heard my brother say, "T.J., this is for you and the rest of them heathens you run around with. You lay one hand on this boy and I'm gonna cut you. You got it?"

T.J. seemed to be pretty clear on the message and it looked like my trouble was over. Of course, that was until my brother, my hero, leaned over to me and said in a whisper, "I'll take care of your black-loving ass when I get you home."

When I got home that afternoon nothing was said about the encounter. I waited all day that day and the next, yet nothing was said. I knew at some point it was going to happen, but nothing happened until Saturday night, right after we went to bed.

My bed was up in the attic. I pulled the folding steps up after me. I loved that little room up there — it was private, and it was mine. About a half hour later, I heard the stairs being pulled down, and I saw the top of my brother's head as he came up the steps. I knew I was in trouble and just hoped there would be enough left of me to get to church for my sermon the next day.

"Boy, you up here?" he growled, kind of.

I stayed real quiet, but he turned the light on and there I was with no place to go. He came over and sat on the side of my bed. We just sat there for a minute with neither one of us saying anything.

The he broke the silence, "You still gonna preach down at Mr. Moses church tomorrow?"

"Yea, if you don't kill me tonight."

He just kind of laughed under his breath, "I ain't gonna kill you. I don't hardly know how to say this, but I guess I'm sort of proud of you. Never thought you would hold out and do it. Been pretty rough these last few days, ain't it been?"

"Could of been worse, I reckon. It got a lot better when you took on T.J. Lord, I thought I was dead on that one."

"Been wanting to show that sum-bitch a few things for a year or two. You just give me an excuse to."

I decided I might as well get on with it, whatever it was. No use in being scared any longer. "Well, whatever you got to say or do, do it. I need to get to sleep if I'm gonna preach for three hours tomorrow."

He laughed and it was a friendly sort of laugh like other brothers share sometime. "I ain't really got nothing to say. Just thought I'd let you know I'm gonna come with Mama and Daddy tomorrow to the black church to hear you preach. I been givin' you a pretty rough time myself so's the least I can do is come cheer you on. Give me the nod and I'll give you an amen from time to time. Lord, knows, you gonna need it."

With that he reached over and ruffled my bright red hair, got up, and went down the stairs. He closed the stairs behind him, and I was glad he did. That sorry rascal had just about made me cry. Bless his sorry soul.

Eleven

I BOUGHT A PINK SUIT. I KNOW that sounds crazy, but on the week before I was to preach my second sermon, my mama sent me to town to buy a new suit. The one I wore for my first sermon was a hand-me-down from Danny and I already outgrew it. I tried to tell Mama that before I preached for Bro. Earl Lee, but she didn't believe it until she saw me on the platform that morning with my cuffs four inches above my shoes and my sleeves only slightly below my elbows. Even she was embarrassed. No need to dwell on such things though.

I went to Blytheville, nine miles from Frostbite and the heart of commerce for northeast Arkansas, to the Billard Dry Goods store. I was going to get myself a new suit for my second sermon, and I was going to look some kind of good.

Well, what can I say. "It looked good in the store." Right there among the very conservative black and very distinguished blue pin-striped suits, I spotted the pink one. The salesman called it a soft rose, but anyone with two eyes could see it was pink.

Since I was also playing in a jazz combo at school, I just figured this suit would cover two purposes. I could look good in the jazz group and I would stand out in the pulpit. Shoot, why try to defend my stupid decision to buy a pink suit? It was made with the same forethought I gave to dying my hair green with Rite permanent dye when I was in the fourth grade. I didn't know you were supposed to use food color, so I used Rite and my hair was green for three months. And my suit was pink for two years before I outgrew it.

Remember the black and pink phase of the Elvis era? I fit right into that period of time, I just went a little overboard on the pink. I did buy a nice black shirt and topped it all off with a black-and-pink polka dot tie. I looked like an idiot, but I was a stylish idiot.

Before I left the store, they insisted on hemming the cuffs and cutting off the sleeves to ensure a proper fit. This gave absolute assurance that I could not return the suit and get my mama's hard-earned money back. Looking back on it, I have the distinct impression that the store manager knew if he didn't fit it to me at that moment, my mama would have it back on his rack before the sun went down. So for better or for worse, I had one fine pink suit.

It looked worse when Mama opened the box and looked at it. Her only comment was, "Well, they sure ain't gonna use you for no funeral preaching." Shaking her head she just went back to the kitchen. Then she yelled back at me, "You might want to hide that thing before your daddy comes home."

I did.

So the first time anyone saw me in my fashionable new pink suit was when I got dressed for church on Sunday morning and walked out to get in the truck. My brother, that sorry good for nothing heathen, took one look and almost fell out of the truck laughing.

Daddy turned to see what he was laughing at and got as red in the face as I had ever seen him. "Well, they ain't gonna confuse you with Bro. Earl Lee today. That's for damn sure." He was not smiling when he said that. "Get in the car boy, let's all go make redneck fools out of ourselves."

What a fine beginning to the day. I looked like Elvis. I was going to preach in the black church, and my last sermon had lasted five minutes. Lord, I couldn't wait for the day to get rolling.

The service at the First Baptist Church started at 11:30 AM. A lot of the black people had to work on Sunday mornings so they started the service late to accommodate everyone. Over at the white Frostbite Baptist Church, Sunday school started at 9:45 AM with the preaching service starting at 11 AM. That worked in my favor because "our folks" would still be in church when the service started over at "their church" where I was preaching. This also worked to my advantage because, at best, I could only make a fool out of myself in front of about 75 black people. I knew they would be kind enough to not talk about me all week even if they did think I was a sorry representation of the Gospel.

Rev. Moses, or as he was called on Sunday, the Rev. and Most Holy and Apostolic Moses R. Johnson, had passed the word around town that anyone who wanted to come to the service was welcome. He said it was going to be a fine day and that the church would prepare dinner on the grounds for anyone who attended. That word went out to all the white churches in town, but I knew that would not help attendance. There was no way folks were going to miss going to their own church and get out at noon in time to have Sunday dinner at Miss Hawkins' BBQ place to go to the black church to hear me preach and not get out until the Cardinals had been beaten by the White Sox late that afternoon.

When we rolled up to the church I realized I miscalculated the desire of the people of Frostbite, Arkansas, to see the "boy" make a fool out of himself one more time. In a small town, you get to know what kind of car or truck people drive. Besides all the normal "about to fall apart and head for the junkyard stuff" that most of the townspeople drove, there were just some that stood out.

I saw Darnel Rosebud's red Chevrolet. Darnel was a deacon at our church so I knew the Frostbite Baptist Church would have a spy in the crowd. There, parked by Mr. R.C's grocery store, was Mary Ann Nedworth's new blue Buick with chrome wheels. The first chrome wheels in the county, I might add. Mary Ann went to the Church of Christ. Chalk up one for the mystery crowd. Then Tyrone Lesterbutt's red Buick with the white trim was parked up by the church. Mr. Lesterbutt was a big dog at the Methodist Church, so by my count every church in town was covered.

Then I spotted it, sort of parked over to the side and about halfway in the ditch. There was Mr. Ledbetter's big black Cadillac. Even that sorry, godless rich man couldn't pass up the opportunity to come to the show even if it was in a black church.

Consider that most folks lived less than four blocks from the church and might have had an opportunity to walk to church, I was beginning to get the impression that I might be a bigger draw than I thought. Just as we drove up, Jasper Smith, one of the deacons there at the church, met us even before Daddy could get the truck parked.

"Over here, Mr. Elroy. We got a special parking place for the Reverend and his family. Y'all just follow me over here and I'm aiming to get you parked right up close." He started clearing folks out of the way and before we knew it, we were parked right up by the side door.

Jasper was still in charge, "Now, Mr. Elroy, you and Miss Martha and your other boy here, will be ushered by Sister Willie May down to the honored seat on the front row. I'm gonna take the Reverend here 'round to the reverend entrance at the back door. The Rev. and Most Holy and Apostolic Moses R. Johnson gonna be waiting for the young reverend there in the back of the church where they gonna do some praying before the service begins."

So off I went with Jasper to the reverend entrance. He just opened the door and sort of pushed me in the room. Standing there in all his "reverend splendor" was the Rev. Moses. He was dressed up something fine that day, just like I was. He was all dressed in black, a snow white tie accompanied by a matching white handkerchief, and his white spats covered his black patent leather shoes just as they did every Sunday. He took one look at me and leaned back and started laughing like I had never heard him laugh before.

"I tell you the truth, Bro. Sam. One thing is for sure, they ain't gonna get us mixed up today. You looks a whole lot like an evangelist. You didn't tell me you was gonna be no evangelist, I might have taught you some different kind of preaching things." By then tears were flowing and he pulled out his big white handkerchief and blew his nose and wiped his eyes. "Lord, Lord, we gonna have us a time today just preaching and praising Jesus."

When he had composed himself a bit, he got back to serious business. We were going to stay here at the back of the church until the service was rolling along. Then after Sister Miltilda Ulah Knox, the Rev. Moses sister, had sung the special hymn solo, we were then going to make our entrance. He warned me that in a black church things were a little different than in a white church. "Don't be surprised if things are rocking a little by the time we get there," he cautioned. "Of course, in your Elvis outfit, you look like you might just do a little rocking for Jesus yourself." This statement brought on another round of uncontrolled laughter.

"By the way, I'm gonna introduce you and I'm gonna set you up for laying the Word on them this fine Sunday. But after that, the service is yours. If you go 10 minutes or two hours, it don't make no difference 'cause when you through, we gonna go outside and eat some chicken. I ain't one to mess with the Lord's Word like Bro. Earl Lee did after you got through preaching at his church last time."

All I heard was "when you through, we gonna go outside and eat some chicken." I had a panic feeling right at that moment that we very well might beat all the other churches to Miss Hawkins' BBQ after all. Unless they did a powerful lot of singing, this service was gonna finish up pretty quick if I was true to form.

Sister Miltilda Ulah Knox, better known as Millie through the week when she was the maid for Mr. Ledbetter, did do a fine job of getting folks in the mood for some Gospel preaching. She let loose with "Come Down Jesus" and, by the time she got through with the second verse, the folks were clapping and praising the Lord something fierce.

That place was really rocking! On the very last verse, Rev. Moses took me by the arm and off we went to make our grand entrance.

Just as Millie, I'm sorry, just as Sister Knox hit her last note, the good Reverend and I were standing on the platform looking out at about everybody in town. I mean that place was full with some people about hanging out the windows.

I would have to say we were talking about 200 folks, which if my calculation is right, is about 30 more than the entire population of Frostbite, Arkansas, sitting out there praising the Lord together. I'm talking white folks and black folks sitting side by side just clapping and laughing and praising and calling out for Sister Knox to sing one more verse.

Rev. Moses called her up there and told her to let loose with one more verse and that is exactly what she did. And just as she launched into the highest notes I ever heard under heaven, I heard that same little voice I had heard right at the start of my first sermon. That little voice was saying, "Sam, my man, it is about time you let your bladder get a little relief."

Sister is singing and I'm praying. I don't know whether I was praying to the Lord or praying to that little voice, but I was saying under my breath, "Lord, don't do this to me again." And right back came that little voice saying, "Boy, don't mess with me 'cause I need to pee right now!"

Sister is singing, Rev. Moses is praising the Lord, and I am about to pee in my pants. I leaned over and pulled on Rev. Moses' coat. He stops singing and leans his head down to me and I told him of the voices I was hearing. Without missing a beat he whispered in my ear, "Know the problem exactly so here's what we gonna do. I'm gonna have Sister sing another verse and you go outside and let it go. We ain't got no facilities, but just find you two big cars, get between them, and let loose. Don't be long cause she's already about to bust something on them high notes."

Just as she stopped singing and the crowd started to settle down, Rev. Moses got their attention, "Listen up now. Y'all all listen up. Ain't no doubt the Lord is using Sister Miltilda in a mighty way, so I wants all of us to close our eyes and let her sing one more verse real slow-like. We got to settle this thing down some before this young reverend here," he placed his hand on my shoulder, "comes and lays the Word of the Lord on us. Now close them eyes and let's get ready for one last verse."

Just as they closed their eyes, he shoved me toward the door and I headed out. "Come Down Jesus" was just a short little song and I didn't have time to be messing around. I found Mr. Rosebud's car crunched up against the building and I started responding to the voice I had heard within. Though the window, I heard Rev. Moses start talking just as Sister Knox was finishing up on that high note that only she could hit.

"Now, let's all just keep our eyes closed for a minute. I think the Lord's got something for us this morning, but for right now, I don't want nobody looking around."

As I opened the door where we entered some 20 minutes before, I saw him frantically motioning me to get up beside him. I looked out and he still had everyone's eyes closed and every head bowed. Even my brother, that infidel, had his eyes closed and didn't know I had taken a slight detour on my way to the pulpit. Just as I got settled in, Rev. Moses starts talking,

"Folks, it's mighty good to see everybody here today. Hope we got enough fried chicken for this big crowd. What you think Sister Willie May, we gonna be able to feed all these folks?"

Sister Willie May stuck her head from around the corner where the deaconesses were sitting and yelled back, "Reverend, you worry about the preaching and all us deaconesses gonna worry about the chicken. I reckon we can take care of everybody." Everybody, black and white, roared with laughter. Without a doubt, folks were having a good time.

I looked at my watch and saw that it was already 12:20 and I hadn't preached a lick. Rev. Moses was doing some filling in just in case I came up with another five-minute masterpiece. I appreciated every minute he took out of my time. He was in his element and was acknowledging all the distinguished people present.

"Mr. Ledbetter, Lord, it is nice to see you here today. I think the Lord just might do something in your soul before this day is over." The entire crowd roared with laughter again, even Mr. Ledbetter. "And Mr. R.C, good to see you here. Before this day is over, we may have to ask you to open that store up and let me box up some more chicken for this bunch. Since you good at selling and I'm good at boxing, I believe we may just be able to feed the whole bunch."

"I told you don't worry about the chicken, Moses. Just get the sermon going and leave the chicken to us!" That was Sister Willie May protecting her territory. This brought the house down with laughter again. I'm here to tell you I was about to get in the swing of things myself. I was laughing and clapping and couldn't wait till Rev. Moses got through so I could lay into them. But he kept talking, "Well, we got a fine treat in store for us today. I believe y'all know Dr. Sam Hamilton, who is the son of Mr. Elroy and Mrs. Martha, who are sittin' right here on the front row with us today."

"Rev. Moses," I whispered loud enough for him to hear me and lean over to see what I had to say. "Rev. Moses, I ain't no doctor. Don't be callin' me no doctor. I got enough problems being a reverend."

"Hush, boy. In our church, every time a visiting preacher comes, we call him doctor. Now you just gonna have to do it our way." He turned back to the congregation.

"Bro. Sam just wanted me to know he was about ready to let loose, so if I could hurry it up he would appreciate it." Again they clapped and laughed. Only this time I think they were laughing at me instead of with me.

Just as he started to complete his introduction, he stopped in midsentence. From where I was sitting, I didn't know what was happening, but it had to be serious because the whole crowd went quiet.

"Bro. Earl Lee, it is fine to see you come join us. Must of got out early down at your church this morning. Come on up here and sit with me and the young reverend. In a minute, I want you to lay a hand on him and pray for him before he preaches to us. You don't mind doing that, do you?"

I heard Bro. Earl Lee mumbling something and then he came up and sat down beside me. He didn't look at me or anything, just sat there looking out at all his members who went to the black church for the service that day, turned out only 11 people showed up for his. So the man was not in the mood to be laying hands on me unless those hands were around my throat.

But Rev. Moses plodded on, "Jesus was just a boy the first time He went to the Temple and preached to all the people. Well, Dr. Sam is just a boy too. Now that means he probably gonna make some mistakes. That's fine we gonna look past the mistakes at what the Lord is trying to do with him. I told him we got all day if he wants to preach all day." I heard most of the white folks groan and most of the black folks shout amen. There was a very distinct difference in the level of enthusiasm exhibited by both races.

Rev. Moses continued, "But however long he preaches, whatever he says is gonna be from God and we gonna listen and urge him on. Dr. Sam, these is fine folks out here. Most of us been watching you grow from a child baby to where you are today and we gonna amen you and praise the Lord for you whether you take five minutes or five hours. But before you come, I want Dr. Earl Lee to come and say a prayer on you."

I looked over at Bro. Earl Lee and he was not moving. Just like me he heard "doctor" and just figured Rev. Moses was talking about someone else. Finally I nudged him, and he looked up and saw Rev. Moses looking at him. Suddenly he got the point and jumped up and yanked me up with him. Putting on his best preacher voice, he slapped one hand on my head and let loose praying.

"Lord, this is the boy you sent to preach to us today. Now we ain't expecting much so whatever you do with him, we ain't gonna be disappointed. So such as he is, use him for Your glory. Amen and amen, now boy, it is all yours." And he sat down.

It was my moment and, unlike my time before the Frostbite Baptist Church, I suddenly realized I was not afraid. For fear my daddy would run up to the pulpit and jerk them out of my hands, I did not have any notes. Just my big red letter Bible and all Bro. Moses' coaching. I was ready to lay it on them as any country preacher would say and I was ready to lay it on good because Rev. Moses had been sharpening my ax for the past few weeks. I knew in my soul I was ready to chop wood for the Lord. Without any hesitation, I jumped right in.

Mama made Daddy bring the wire recorder again even though he protested and used all sorts of excuses to leave it home. So right up there on the pulpit, there was the microphone that scared me to death at the white church. Here in this setting, I saw it as a friend and I reached over and turned it on. These are the words that were recorded that day in a black church in Frostbite, Arkansas, when the Lord laid His hand on me for the very first time:

Good morning. I'm glad everyone came to church today to hear this humble preacher try to preach the Word of the Lord to you. I realize that in my first attempt not much came of it, and I rightly admit I didn't know what I was doing. But since that time, I been spending some time with Rev. Moses out under the tree in front of Mr. R.C.'s store, and I've learned a few things about preaching.

I looked at Bro. Earl Lee and he was so red in the face he was about to bust. Daddy had his head down and Mama was shaking her head back in forth warning me that I was on dangerous ground. The rest of the church just sat in stone silence. Even Bro. Moses refrained from his usual "Thank you, Lord" as he saw his job at Mr. R.C.'s store fall into jeopardy. I moved on.

I learned that ain't no preaching any good if the Lord don't lay His hand on you first, so I want y'all to all pray that today the Lord will lay His hand on me.

I don't have to tell you I'm bad scared. My heart is beating fast and both hands is full of sweat so I need everyone here to pray for me. If you are white, I need you to pray for me. If you are black, I need you to pray for me. If you are red, yellow, blue or green, I need you to pray for me.

See how the rhythm was building up? Suddenly I heard the first "amen" come across and it was from my daddy. I didn't know if he was getting into the swing of things or just realized I needed a lot of praying going on in my behalf. Also, that little bit about the "red, yellow, blue or green" sort of broke the ice and a few people started nudging one another and laughing a little. I was getting to them, and I was greatly encouraged.

Last week I was trying to decide what to preach about and I decided to just preach about Jesus. We done heard enough about the prophets. We done heard enough about the disciples. We done heard enough about the problems of the world as great as they may be. What we ain't heard enough about is Jesus.

To his credit, Bro. Earl Lee jumped straight up and yelled, "Preach on, boy. Talk to us." When that happened, I knew I was getting through. His affirmation just set off another round of amens that were going to stay steady with me for the next hour. Lord, this was getting to be fun!

I ask you today, Who is this Jesus that I preach about on this fine Sunday morning in Mississippi County, Arkansas? Is He just another man who walked the earth? Talk to me! I say, Is He just a man who walked the earth?

Rev. Moses came up out of his seat and shouted, "No, sir, Reverend. He is not just another man!" When he did that, every black person in the place started shouting and praising the Lord the likes of which I had never heard. Now with Bro. Earl Lee's permission and Rev. Moses' permission, everyone in the house was getting into it. This was going to be a fine day.

Y'all right. Jesus is not just a man who walked this earth 2,000 years ago. Who is He then? I ask you, Who is He if He is not just a man? Well, let me tell you who He is. He is the first and the last, the beginning and the end. That's who He is. Long before Moses was on the mountain, Jesus was with the Father. Long before Elijah built the fire at Mt. Carmel, Jesus was in existence. Long before the angels came and announced His birth, Jesus was alive and well. I say, long before Mr. Ledbetter ever ginned his first bale of cotton, Jesus was planting the seed of the Kingdom.

Folks fell in the floor at the use of Mr. Ledbetter's name. I could also tell by looking at him he was a little pleased to be recognized. Things were rolling. It was time to start using some of Rev. Moses' connectors.

Y'all know it's true. Give Jesus a hand! He was here from the beginning and He is here today in our midst. Thank you, Jesus. Say Amen!

Who is this Jesus? He is the keeper of the Creation, and the Creator of all. Sometimes we think we make something fine, but Jesus is the fine maker. Sometimes we think we make the cotton grow, but Jesus is the keeper of the growing. Last year, the Mississippi River rose up and flooded our town and now they is building a big levee to hold the water back. We don't need no levee, we just need Jesus to take His finger and make the river deeper 'cause Jesus is the Creator of it all. He does little things that we think is big and He does big things that we think is little. The Bible says that not a sparrow falls that He does not know about. Jesus created it from the beginning and from the beginning it was His. I said it once and now I say it twice, long before Mr. Ledbetter ever ginned his first bale of cotton, Jesus was planting the seed of the Kingdom.

Later my Grandma said I got a little carried away on the levee stuff. Her house had almost washed away last year and she was a mite touchy about the levee. But anyway, I was on a roll and the people were with me. Rev. Moses' rhythm stuff was paying off.

Clap your hands for Jesus and say Amen!

I ask you again, who is this Jesus? He is the Architect of the universe and the Manager of all times. Three years ago, Mr. Ledbetter built that big house out on his plantation. He brought in an architect from Memphis to make the plans and oversee the building of that fine house of his. Most of us thought that was really something. But let me tell you something big. Something big was when Jesus designed the universe with all its stars and all its wonders. Something big was when Jesus flung the stars into place and lifted the mountains from the plains.

Let me read you something from the book of Joshua, Joshua 10:12-13, read it with me:

"Then spake Joshua to the LORD in the day when the LORD delivered up the Amorites before the children of Israel, and he said in the sight of Israel, Sun, stand thou still upon Gibeon; and thou, Moon, in the valley of Ajalon.

"And the sun stood still, and the moon stayed, until the people had avenged themselves upon their enemies."

Is not this written in the book of Joshua? So the sun stood still in the midst of heaven, and hasted not to go down about a whole day.

Something big was when Jesus made the sun stand still for Joshua. Something big was when He rose from the dead.

I see Bro. Webb is here from the Methodist church. Last year Bro. Webb got stuck in Jerry Stillman's new car. Had to tow him into town to get him out. Most of us think Bro. Webb is big, but he ain't nothing compared to Jesus. Jesus is the biggest of the biggest. Bro. Webb, he makes you look like a midget.

Say Amen! 'cause you know it's true!

Bro. Webb jumped up and almost knocked the pew over. He was shouting and laughing with everyone else. For a few minutes I swear he forgot he was a Methodist. Lord, we were having a good time. Now I had Bro. Earl Lee, Rev. Moses, and Bro. Webb all shouting and saying Amen. I figured I was pushing my luck on the Church of Christ. I didn't know his name, and if he was there, I don't think he was into the swing of things at this point.

Jesus is the Manager of all time. He sat with the Father when the day was divided from the night. He sat with the Father when in six days the heavens and the earth were made. And on the seventh day, He sat with the Father and had a cup of cool iced tea and looked around and said, "This looks pretty good. I think we done us a pretty good job."

Put your hands together and say Amen for Jesus who is the Manager of all time.

I have no idea where all that stuff was coming from. To say the least, I was no authority on the Trinity. Until later in my seminary work, I had never heard the whole story about the Lord making the sun stand still. But the folks were into it, and I could tell Rev. Moses knew what he was talking about when he said if the Lord was upon you, the people would preach you to death. They were just easing out of the last hand-clapping when I started up again.

Talk to me now! Who is this Jesus? He always was, He always is, and He always will be ... Unmoved, Unchanged, Undefeated, and never Undone. That's who He is!

He always was. Before we got up this morning, Jesus was already up and rolling. Before my grandma was born, Jesus was already there. Jesus always is. Now listen to me on this one. Jesus gonna be here a long time after we all gone. You know what I mean? The armies may try to run Him out. But He is always here. They may try to drop one of them atomic bombs on Him, but Jesus is always here. And not only that, Jesus will always be. You may not let Him live in your heart, but that's okay. He is still gonna be somewhere. You may hide and you may run, but Jesus is always gonna be 'round.

He is unmoved. When Satan took Him into the mountain and tried to buy Him off, Jesus was not moved to accept. When Judas gave Him the devil's kiss, Jesus did not raise a hand to retaliate. Jesus never moves from His position of right. My daddy bought a new tractor last year. It's a big tractor with a powerful motor. But tie that tractor to my Jesus and that tractor gonna bog down, 'cause Jesus can't be moved.

Say Amen! for the unmovable Jesus.

Jesus in unchanged. Jesus don't wear no white hat one day and no black hat the next. He is always the same. You ask Jesus a question today and ask him that same question 10,000 years from now, He gonna tell you the same answer, 'cause Jesus is always the same. I don't know about you folks, but I like a Jesus that is unchanged.

Jesus is undefeated, and never undone. Bring on your armies. He'll stand against you. Bring on your navy and he'll sink your ships. Try to trick Him up and He will catch you in the act. Shoot at Him with your biggest gun and He will catch the bullet in His teeth. Mr. Truman dropped them bombs on Japan and the world thought that was power. Mr. Hitler took them armies all over the land and thought that was power. But let me tell you one thing I don't want you to forget. You ain't seen power until you seen the power of Jesus. That Man is undefeated, and never undone.

Put your hands together for our undefeated Jesus.

Whee, I tell you it's getting' hot in here ain't it? Y'all excuse me whilst I take this coat off. Lord, I'm about to die of the heat. By the way, what y'all think about my pink suit? My mama says I look like a ball of cotton candy, but I sort of like it. What you folks think about it?

The crowd went wild again as the church was filled with good-hearted laughter. Later Rev. Moses said he had never seen black folks and white folks in the same room having such a good time. He also said my comment about the pink suit was just at the right time. "Sometime when the Spirit is moving you, you got to calm 'em down. That pink suit comment seemed to do that." Anyway, I moved on.

Now let's get back to Jesus. Who is this Jesus? He was bruised and brought healing! He was pierced and eased pain? Just think about it. The Bible says "He was bruised for our iniquity." No one suffered more for us, and yet while He walked on this earth and since He went back to be with the Father, He has brought healing to our souls. They let down a leper into the room that was so crowded they could not get him in to see Jesus. Tore off the roof, I'm here to tell you. Tore it right off so he could see Jesus. Now if the roof was tore off this church today, most of us would be scared. If the roof fell in, most of us would run. But when the roof fell in and a poor leper dropped to the floor, our Jesus healed him and sent him home. Jesus always brings about healing.

Y'all remember that bad cat fight Miss Ruth had with Miss Foster down at the hair parlor last year 'bout this time? Y'all remember that? Then you remember how we had that revival in the fall and Bro. Williams from Lepanto came over and preached the Gospel. Then you remember on that last night when Miss Ruth and Miss Foster met at the altar and were hugging and kissing and making up 'cause Jesus had come into their hearts. Y'all remember that? That's what Jesus does. He might have been hurting His self, or He might still have been sore from that spear in His side, but Jesus found time to get them two fine women together and now jes' look at them, sitting out here this morning side by side. That's what Jesus does when something needs to be healed.

He was pierced and eased pain. I ain't hardly old enough to shave, but a few weeks ago I picked up my daddy's straight razor and near 'bout cut my finger off. Still hurts to this day.

It was the middle finger on my right hand, and I held it up for everyone to see how it was healed. Just as I got it in the air, it dawned on me I was giving all the good people of Frostbite, Arkansas, the "bird" in the name of Jesus so I got it right back down, only not before old Leroy, who once again found a front-row seat, let out a belly laugh you could have heard in Jonesboro. But I digress. Back to the preaching.

My hurt finger wasn't nothing compared to the nails in His hands and feet and the spear in His side. But while folks back then did that to Jesus, He was just going on about His business healing folks and making them well.

I look out here and I see Sister Willie May. Sister Willie May came down with the gout last summer. Couldn't hardly walk. But Jesus healed her bad foot. Ain't that right, Sister Willie May?

I see my Aunt Rosy out there. Aunt Rosy, up till about two years ago, had a bad heart. Went down to Memphis and got it worked on. Now she goes about her business like nothing was ever wrong. That was Jesus healed that heart, Aunt Rosy. That was Jesus. Jesus is in the healing business even though sometimes He is bruised and tired.

Let's give Jesus a hand for being in the healing business. Some of the rest of us gonna need His healing touch so let's give Jesus a hand in advance.

Who is this Jesus? He was persecuted and brought freedom. He was dead and brought life. They threw Him in jail. They put chains on His hands and His feet. They tried to tie Him up and hold Him down, but in spite of that, Jesus was there to set them free. That's the way Jesus works. Jesus is in the settin' free business.

He was dead and brought life. Old Lazarus was in that tomb. Been there three days and smelled real bad. His sister is walking around crying 'cause her little brother had died. She kept saying, "If Jesus was just here, my brother would still be alive." 'Bout that time Jesus showed up. Jesus said, "Where is that tomb?" Some man pointed and said, "Over there where that bad smell is coming from."

Jesus walked over and told old Lazarus to wake up and come on out. And the Bible says that's what happened. Lazarus just got up off that tomb floor and, with his grave clothes still on his back, he walked out and lived again. That's what Jesus did. Jesus brought life and He still does.

I got me an uncle and if I called his name, y'all would all know who I am talking about. Couldn't be here today 'cause he is in the hospital. But my uncle was a drunk. The devil rum got in his soul and he was a walking dead man. But in that revival I mentioned a while ago, he came to Jesus. He walked out to his car and pulled out a whiskey bottle and threw it as far as he could. Far as I know he ain't touched a drop since, and he has had a year of life with Jesus. That's who Jesus is. Jesus is the One who brings life.

If you believe it, say Amen!

Who is this Jesus we talking about this morning? He is risen and brings power. He reigns and brings peace. That's the Jesus I'm talking about. They thought they could take away His power by hanging Him on a cross. They thought they could take away His power by gambling for His clothes. They thought they could take away His power by persecuting His followers. But on the third day, death could not hold Him. The darkness could not shut out His light. And on the third day, He arose again in all His power.

He could have used that power to trample on His enemies. He could have knocked the Romans soldiers back into history. He could have brought kings down from their thrones. But instead, He came back as the Prince of Peace. When Jesus reigns there is peace like no peace you have ever known. That's the Jesus we talking about.

Say Amen! if you believe Jesus is the Prince of Peace!

By now I had the rhythm Bro. Moses had talked about. I understood what he meant when he said that it was important from time to time to stop the rhythm method of preaching and give the folks a pause. "Don't want nobody to get worked up and have a heart attack, you know." So I decided I better calm things down a bit. I took my handkerchief out of my pocket and wiped my face all over. It was about 100 degrees in the church and this church was a long way from having air conditioning.

Y'all gonna have to excuse me a minute while I cool down. I tell you, I've picked cotton and boxed strawberries, but I do believe you get hotter preaching the Gospel than 'bout anything I've done.

Laughter throughout the crowd. I made the most of it by drinking down a big glass of water that one of the deaconesses brought up to the pulpit. I forgot about my previous urinary tract urgencies and was just glad to get the water. As soon as I sat the glass down, I turned around like I was whispering something to Rev. Moses. He just gave me a "preach on, brother" and I suddenly whirled around and shouted.

I ASK YOU AGAIN. WHO IS THIS JESUS WE TALKING ABOUT TODAY?

All I know is the world can't understand Him, and the armies can't defeat Him.

I went up to the Blytheville library the other day. They got a lot of books up there, all divided up into different sections. All the books on cows are over in one spot and all the books on religion are in another. Well that was the first time I had every been in a library except the one down at the school, so I was pretty impressed. I went over to the section on religion.

Lord, I had never seen so many books. I counted over a hundred before I stopped counting. Seems like everybody has something to say about Jesus. It's like they are trying to figure Him out or something. Well I'm here to tell you that you don't need no hundred books about Jesus. No sir, you just need one book. And it is this Book. Maybe the reason so many people are confused about things today is they been reading the wrong book. No sir, the world can't understand this Man who was the Son of God. So when they couldn't understand Him, they decided to destroy Him.

But, even armies can't destroy Him. Hitler tried and look where he is today. He had a lot of tanks and guns and bombs. He tried to wipe out the people of God, but he got wiped out instead. You don't mess with Jesus. Jesus says, "Bring on your biggest army. I'll take you on. You can't beat me!" That's who Jesus is.

Let me tell you something else. The schools can't explain Him and the universities can't ignore Him. Lord knows, I am glad I live in this great state of Arkansas. I heard on the news the other night about a school up there in New York or somewhere that had decided that they ought to close down a student prayer meeting that was being held on the school yard after school. The superintendent said he didn't want nothing going on he couldn't explain, and since he couldn't understand or explain praying to Jesus then they couldn't meet. Them folks need to get them another superintendent. Down here in Arkansas, our superintendents understand Jesus.

Universities can't ignore Him. Y'all read about that flap at the University of Arkansas last year. Group of them commie teachers, or professors I think they call them, decided to stop teaching a course on the life of Jesus. Well, they forgot where they were. They weren't in no Yankee university where God ain't allowed. No sir, they were in the South where God is King and the Board of Trustees 'bout came unglued. Took about two minutes to get Jesus back on the calendar at good old Razorback University. The message they got was you can't ignore Jesus.

Let's put our hands together and say, "Souie pigs! And thank you, Jesus! Amen! Amen!"

Now let's just get back to Bible time for a minute. Who is this Jesus? He is a man who Herod couldn't kill, the Pharisees couldn't confuse, and the people couldn't hold. That's who Jesus is!

When Jesus was born, old Herod got a little upset because wise men were running around saying that this baby was the promised Messiah. He would be King of the Jews and Lord of Lords. So old Herod came up with a tax idea so he could round people up. Then he decided to just kill all the babies to make certain he got Jesus in the round up. But the angel of the Lord came to Joseph and Mary and told them to go to Egypt and stay. And that is what they did. Try though he might, old Herod couldn't kill Him. Say Amen!

I knew I was getting things a little mixed up from the original Greek and stuff, but I was on a roll and historical details just didn't seem important at the time.

Then Jesus grew up and He started His preaching. A bunch of teachers and preachers thought they were better than Him and would go to the Temple to argue with Him. Jesus never lost. They asked him about taxes and Jesus told them to give to Caesar what was his and to God what was His. They brought a woman before Him and wanted to stone her. Jesus wrote in the sand for the person without sin to throw the first stone and when He looked up they had all gone. The Pharisees couldn't confuse Him. He was on a mission and would not be distracted. Say Amen! for the unconfused Jesus!

And the people couldn't hold him. I don't remember where it is in the Bible, but there came a time when a big mob came after Him to throw Him over a cliff and Jesus just vanished before their eyes. Just became a mist. You can't hold no mist, and He was gone just to show up and preach another day. I like a Jesus the people can't hold but who is willing to hold the people.

Am I preaching or not? Y'all stand up and give Jesus a hand.

I had been going for about 45 minutes and figured I needed to let them stand up and stretch. Also, I knew there were a couple of Episcopalians in the crowd and I figured they probably had about all their behinds could absorb by now. They were worse than the Methodists on getting short sermons, but to my surprise, not a soul left the church.

Who is this Jesus? He is a Man who Nero couldn't crush and the Roman army couldn't silence. He is a Man that that godless Communist bunch can't replace and that new guy on that radio show out of Little Rock can't explain away. Lord, Lord, Lord. Who is this Man? He is Jesus the Son of the Holy God and the strongest and most influential men on this earth can't hold a match to Him.

About that time, Sister Willie May got to shouting. She ran up the aisle of the church and grabbed Rev. Moses and nearly hugged him to death. Folks were clapping and praising the Lord like I never heard.

Before we knew what was happening, Sister Willie May was struck by the Spirit and fell backwards off the platform. Daddy, being on the front row, tried to catch all 400 pounds of her and strained his back. With Sister Willie May on the floor and Daddy holding his back and crying out in pain, we were having some kind of service.

Rev. Moses just whispered in my ear, "Now just let 'em settle down a bit, and then go on preaching. You got the rhythm, Bro. Sam, so just keep on rolling." So I rolled!

Well, I believe Sister Willie May just set the tone for the next thing I want to say about Jesus. Listen up now. Who is this Jesus? He is light, love and longevity. The Bible says, "He is the light of the World." The Bible says, "He is everlasting." The little song we sing in Sunday school says, "Jesus loves me this I know, for the Bible tells me so." He is love in the highest degree.

Who is He? He is goodness, kindness, gentleness and God! Listen to me, we changing gears here. We are moving into holy ground because we are moving toward this man Jesus who is God Himself. In Him is no selfishness, only goodness. In Him is no harshness toward His people, only gentleness. He is like the shepherd who tends his flock and finds one little lamb who has gone astray. He picks that little lamb up and he is gentle with it. When other people are unkind, He is kind.

And when you put the whole package together, He is God. Say Amen if you believe it! He don't ask me to understand it. I don't know how Jesus and the Father can be One. I don't know much about the Holy Spirit and the Father and the Son all being in one Person. There is a whole lot I don't know, but this one thing I do know. Jesus is God. Holy and righteous is He that sits on the throne.

Yes, He is holy, righteous, powerful and pure. When the high priest went into the Holy of Holies, he was there to be in the presence of God. God was there because only He is holy. Jesus is holy. When the armies of Egypt tried to hold back the children of Israel and keep them as slaves, God parted the water of the Red Sea and had them walk across on dry land. God is powerful, therefore Jesus is powerful.

God is pure. When Moses wanted to see Him, God just let Moses see His shadow because God is so pure that the pureness of God would have blinded Moses had he actually seen God. Leastwise I think that was Moses. Might have been someone else, but you get the point. God is pure, therefore Jesus is pure and in Him is no sin. Mighty, righteous, powerful and pure. That's the Jesus we talking about today.

His ways are right, His Word is eternal, His will is unchanging, and His mind is on me. Oh, hang on now 'cause things about to get good around here. Listen up! His Word is eternal. Whatever Jesus says lasts forever. He says, "I am the light of the world" and that light's gonna shine forever because Jesus is eternal. Eternal means a long time.

Sometimes Mrs. Templeton gives us an English test and I think it is going to last forever. Sometimes when I am chopping cotton I think the row gonna go on forever. Sometimes when I was a little kid and my mama used to wash my ears — I thought the washing would go on forever, But none of those things can come close to God's forever. His Word is eternal and that means forever. If He said it in the Old Testament, it is just as true in the New Testament. If He told the crowd they were sinners and He had come to save them, then He is telling us that we are sinners and He has come to save us. Whatever Jesus says is eternal.

His will is unchanging. Jesus won't tell you something today and change His mind tomorrow. You don't ever have to wonder what Jesus is saying or what His will is for you 'cause once you hear Him say it once, you done heard it for eternity.

And His mind is on me. Stop right there cause I'm 'bout to change gears on you one more time. So stay with me. We been talking about Jesus this morning. That's the way it ought to be. But there comes a time when Jesus gets to thinking just about me and you. His mind is not on creating another world. His mind is not on preaching another sermon. His mind is on me and things get serious. So listen close now.

Who is this Jesus? He is my Redeemer, he is my Savior and He is my guide. Sometimes we sing a song about "Redeemed by the Blood of the Lamb." Talk to me now. Who was the Lamb? That's right, the Lamb was Jesus. Say Amen! Whose blood was shed in a sacrifice for us? That's right, it was the blood of the Lamb, and the Lamb is Jesus. So He is my Redeemer.

He is my Savior. We all need a Savior and the Savior we need is Jesus. We are drowning in the lake of sin. Jesus is our Savior. We are falling into the crevice. Jesus is our Savior. We are dying in our sin. Jesus is our Savior. You believe it, say Amen!

Usually by this time in any sermon my daddy would have been asleep. But that day, he was wide awake because you could have set off a bomb in the church and not heard it. I mean, that place was rocking. I had the rhythm going, and the people were getting in the groove. It was something to be a part of this, so early in my ministry.

He is my Redeemer, Savior. He is my Savior, and He is my Guide. You won't ever get lost as long as Jesus is your guide. Say Amen! to that 'cause you know it's true. Last year my friend Bubba and his Daddy went out to Wyoming to shoot elk. They got to this little town in Wyoming and hired them a guide. Only problem was, that guide had only been in Wyoming about two days. No longer than they walked in the woods, they knew they were lost. They looked for moss on the trees and for the North Star, but they were some kind of lost. Took them two days just to get back to the car.

Well, let me tell you something. You won't ever get lost if Jesus is your guide. Every place you want to go, He has already been. No forest is too black, no mountain too high or no valley too low for my Jesus to get lost in. Say Amen!

When we're in the wilderness, He gonna show us the way out. When we don't know which road to take, He gonna read the road map for us. Yes, sir, you better believe it 'cause He is our Redeemer, He is our Savior, and He is our guide. Now put your hands together for the guiding Jesus. And then say Amen!

Who is this Jesus we keep talking about? I'll tell you who He is. He is my peace. When my soul is restless, I can find rest in Him. When the worries of life get me down, He will get me up. I find peace in this man called Jesus. He is my joy. When my soul is in despair and I am at the bottom of the bucket, He makes me laugh and He lifts my spirit.

He is my comfort. When the trials of life start to get me down, I can rest in Him. When tears are in my eyes, He will wipe them away. When my heart is broken, He will rest my head in His lap. Oh, yes, say Amen! 'cause Jesus is our comfort.

But best of all, He is my Lord, and He rules my life! Everybody got a Lord in their life. Some serve demon rum. Some serve snake eyes and box cars at the devil's craps table. Some are ruled by their husband or their wife.

Widespread laughter.

But in my life, He is Lord. He rules my life. He guides my going out and my coming in. Say Amen! 'cause you know it's true.

Now someone might ask, Why would anyone give their life to Jesus to be Lord and Master of their life? Why would anyone turn their life over and have it ruled by someone else even if His name is Jesus? Well, listen up now, 'cause I am going to tell you straight up. I serve Him because His bond is love and His burden is light. I don't serve Him 'cause He has me in chains. I don't' serve Him 'cause He has me in some holy prison. I serve Him because He loves me so much I can do but nothing less. And when I made the decision to follow Him, I found that His burden is light. He carries the load for me. My back never hurts from pulling the sack. My hands never hurt from chopping the row. When I follows Jesus, He takes the burden and makes it light. Say Amen! Say it again, Amen and Amen!

Sister Miltilda fainted. She was probably already weak from hanging on to them high notes so long, but the heat and the preaching got to her and she fell out right off the end of the pew into the aisle.

Sister Willie May was on her like a toad on a rock, splashing water on her face and fanning her with the Blytheville Funeral Home fan.

I was just about to stop when Sister Willie May yelled out, "Don't stop now, Reverend. They is falling one by one!" I preached on.

His goal for me is abundant life. Jesus wants the best for me in every case. I never have to question where He is leading me 'cause He don't want nothing but the best for me. He wants me to have it all.

I follow Him because He is the wisdom of the wise, and the power of the powerful. When I don't know the answer, He has the answer for me. Mrs. Templeton can't give me a test that Jesus don't know the answer to all the questions. When I search for the answers in my life, He comes up with them. He is wise, but He is also powerful.

In fact, He is the power of the powerful. We've just come through a war where Mr. Hitler thought he was powerful, but the Lord showed him real power. Those Japanese dropped their bombs on Pearl Harbor and thought they were powerful. But the Lord showed them what power looked like. And we got to remember that our power, our power as a nation, our power as a people comes not from within ourselves, but it is the power of God within us. Say Amen! You know it's true!

I was beginning to get a little hoarse. All this shouting and preaching and sweating was drying out my voice. Sister Rose Johnson, one of the younger deaconesses, saw what was happening and brought me a glass of water. As she sat it down in front of me, she whispered, "Dr. Sam, you are preaching the Word. We got all day so don't let up." I was reenergized by her encouragement and pressed on.

Let's get back to it now. Sister Rose has brought the water bucket to me and I am tanked up and ready to go.

When the field workers, most of whom were members of this church, worked in the cotton fields, there was always one who brought the water bucket out to give them a drink. When I mentioned the water bucket, you could see I was connecting. Rev. Moses was right. I needed to talk to people about things that were familiar. Everyone loved the water bucket!

I follow Him because He is the Ancient of days, the Ruler of rulers, the Leader of leaders, the Overseer of the overcomers, and the sovereign Lord of all that was .. and is ... and is to come.

Tell me that ain't a Jesus worth following. The Ancient of days. From the beginning He loved us. The Ruler of rulers. Kings bow down and worship him. The Leader of leaders. When the President of the United States takes up the office, he don't put his hand on no comic book. No, sir, he puts his hand on the Bible 'cause he knows Jesus is the Leader of leaders.

He is the Overseer of the overcomers. When that new church was born in Acts chapter two, they had a lot to overcome. Folks wanted to kill them. Folks wanted to persecute them and stomp them down. But Jesus was their Overseer and helped them to overcome. He is the sovereign Lord of all that was ... and is ... and is to come. Stand up right now and praise the Lord. Say Amen! as you do it.

White people were hugging black people and slapping one another on the back. It was something to see. Folks were having a fine time. Even Bro. Earl Lee gave me a thumbs up. I guess I had passed the sermonette stage in his mind.

Now some folks would say at this point that they are impressed with this Jesus I am talking about. But let me tell you right now, there is more to come. Just try this on for size. His goal, I say, His goal is a relationship with me. There came a point where Jesus said, "I don't want to play with the stars no more. I don't need to create any more animals or creatures of the earth. I have made me a man and His name is Sam and he lives in Frostbite, Arkansas, and he is just a boy, but I am willing to give my life to have a relationship with that boy." Lord, Jesus, it don't get no better than that!

Say it with me and put your name in where I put mine. Say it now, "I have made me a man and His name is (put in your own name) and he lives in Frostbite, Arkansas, and he is just a boy, but I am willing to give my life to have a relationship with that boy." Now if you are a woman or a girl, say it again and insert your name. "I have made me a woman and her name is (insert your own name) and she lives in Frostbite, Arkansas, and she is just a girl, but I am willing to give my life to have a relationship with that girl." That's the Jesus I am talking about today.

Now we going into the home stretch. I want y'all to hang on because we coming to the good part. Listen to me now. I just told you, and you just told me, that Jesus wants a relationship with us. Now let me ask you this. Why would we want a relationship with Him. You ready? Let me jes' tell you my reasons and then you can add your own.

I want a relationship with Jesus 'cause He will never leave me. I want a relationship with Jesus 'cause He will never forsake me. Say Amen! You know it's true.

I want a relationship with Jesus 'cause He will never mislead me nor forsake me. I want a relationship with Jesus 'cause He will never forget me, never overlook me, and He will never cancel my appointment in His appointment book.

I want a relationship with Jesus 'cause when I fall, He lifts me up! When I fail, He forgives. When I am weak, He is strong. When I am lost, He is the way.

Y'all gettin' the idea yet? Say Amen! and thank you, Jesus.

I want a relationship with Jesus 'cause when I am afraid, He is my courage. When I stumble, He steadies me. When I am hurt, He heals me. And when I am broken, He mends me.

I want a relationship with Jesus 'cause when I am blind, He leads me on. When I am hungry, He feeds me. When I face trials, He is with me. When they come to persecute me, He is there to shield me. When I face problems, He is there to comfort me!

When I face loss, He provides for me! When I face death, He carries me home. He is everything for everybody, everywhere, every time, and every way. Lord, Jesus, it just don't get no better than this! Say Amen!

He is God, He is faithful. And I am His, and He is mine!

Listen to me. My Father in heaven can whip the father of this world! So if you are wondering why I feel so secure, you just need to understand this ...

He said it and that settles it! God is in control, I am on His side, and that means all is well with my soul. Every day is a blessing 'cause God is, and that settles it!

Amen and amen and amen again! Thank you, Jesus.

Sister Miltilda, I believe you are going to sing us to heaven so come up and let it loose cause this preacher is about preached out.

Sister Miltilda, who by this time had regained herself, came up and let loose with "This World is not my Home." Before she was through, the place was really moving and shaking. Rev. Moses came up and lifted the offering and then had the Benediction.

Then we all moved out onto the church yard where black and white folks all sat down together at a common table and ate some of the best fried chicken in the country. People spent all afternoon coming up and commenting on my sermon.

A fine time was had by all, especially the Rev. and Most Holy and Apostolic Moses R. Johnson, who in his divine wisdom, had the courage to bring this community together to hear a 105-pound white boy preach the Word right here in Frostbite, Arkansas.

Twelve

"Boy, you done good," my daddy said as he put his hand on my shoulder. "Good thing you didn't go another five minutes. Damn near run out of wire on the recorder as it was."

Bro. Earl Lee came over and said he had a few places he wanted me to preach over the next few months. He seemed mighty proud of his protégé.

Rev. Moses, just every once in a while, yelled out, "Y'all all ready to go in and let Dr. Sam preach some more?" The crowd would let out a yell and I almost thought I was gonna have to do it all over again.

It was a glorious day and, as the afternoon came to an end, Mr. Ledbetter made his way over to where I was sitting. "Boy, I'm gonna be driving you home today. I done talked to your Daddy, so when you ready, just go over there and get in the car. I'll be ready to go any time you are."

Oh, Lord, I knew I shouldn't have used his name in my sermon. No telling what he was gonna do to me. But Daddy had already agreed, so I made my good-byes and went over and got in Mr. Ledbetter's car. Almost everyone else was already gone, so he just pulled right out on the street and started driving me home. We were moving at a steady five miles per hour.

We drove on out of town, crossing Morgan's Creek on the way to my house. I still didn't know why he wanted to drive me home, so I figured the best thing I could do was just keep my mouth shut.

Just as we turned into the driveway, he spoke up. "You believe that stuff you preached today?"

"Yes, sir, I reckon I do."

"Well, you done real good. Who taught you all that stuff? Went a whole lot better today than it did when you preached for Earl Lee."

I told him about spending time with Rev. Moses. I didn't know what would come of my telling him, but I figured he was gonna know anyway.

There was a long pause, then he said, "Well, he's a good man and he done a good job on you. Now just let me give you a little personal advice if you don't mind.

"Today was a fine day and I think everybody enjoyed they selves real good. But you got to be careful about associatin' with too many of them nigger churches. First thing you know, won't no white church have you preach and you ain't gonna get rich in no black church. You know what I mean?"

I explained that I did, but that I didn't think I was gonna get rich in any white church either. He just sort of grunted as we pulled up in front of my house. He paused a minute and then, with his hands still on the steering wheel and his eyes starring out the windshield he said, "Boy, if you don't mind, I wish you would pray for me when you get time. I'm getting old and I ain't settled nothing up with the Lord yet. Reckon I done enough He might not want me, but I reckon I ought to start getting things settled. Now don't go round telling everybody in town that I ask you to do no praying. You just keep this between you, me and the Lord. Like I said, you done good today. Now get out of here and go on home."

I thanked him for the ride and went in the house. Mama and Daddy and my brother had not made it home because they were going to stop by Aunt Rosy's house. So I went up to my little room in the attic, pulled the stairs up after me, and lay down on my bed.

What a day it had been. When I was up in that pulpit I felt like the Lord Himself was on my shoulder. All those words of praise and encouragement were ringing in my ears. I had heard the people saying *Amen!* to my preaching. I had heard old Mr. Ledbetter asking me to pray for him. I had heard Bro. Earl Lee telling me he was going to get me more places to preach.

I heard a lot of things that day, which became one of the most memorable of my life. The only thing I had not heard was the voice of God calling me to preach the Word. That one thing I really needed, I neither felt nor heard. I had the feeling I could do the job, what I missed was hearing the call. With an emptiness still in my soul, I drifted off to sleep.

Thirteen

It was the summer before my sophomore year in high school when I preached those first two sermons in Frostbite, Arkansas. It was a glorious summer and probably the last I would enjoy as just a kid in high school. After launching my preaching career, even my classmates treated me a little differently. The girls liked me more and the boys tried to tempt me more. I got in my share of trouble and usually got out without much punishment because people always said that "his heart is in the right place."

Bro. Earl Lee decided that there *was* some preaching in me so, after the sermon at Rev. Moses' church, I stayed pretty much booked up. There was only one Sunday from the beginning of my sophomore year until my graduation from high school when I was not preaching for someone, those little country churches with 10 to 100 members.

One cold winter night, I preached at the Half Moon Baptist Church. The temperature outside was about 5 degrees and the wind was blowing from the north. Had we known about wind chill factors in those days, we would have frozen to death that night. Still, about 15 people came to church to hear me preach.

The church was heated by a big wood-burning stove that sat in one corner of the auditorium. We all pulled our chairs up to the fire and sang a couple of songs. I then preached my second shortest sermon, this one lasting about four minutes. Everyone said it was the most wonderful sermon they ever heard. I noticed I got that comment a lot when I came in under 10 minutes.

All my preaching was done in white Baptist churches, usually within about 50 miles or so from my home. I wanted to preach in some more black churches, but did not have an opportunity to do so until I was almost through college. I talked to Rev. Moses about it and he thought things were heating up a little too much on the race issue for me to take a chance on preaching for him again.

The catalyst for the animosity seemed to be the Supreme Court of the United States. It was during my high school years that the Warren Court would hand down their Brown *vs.* the Board of Education opinion saying that "separate but equal" was not equal at all. Integration was to be the social issue of the day and in northeast Arkansas, much like many other places in both the North and the South, things got ugly.

During my high school years, Gov. Orval Faubus of Arkansas sent the state police in to stop integration at Central High School in Little Rock. Another preacher by the name of Dr. Martin Luther King was carrying out a nonviolent approach to integration. It was a good idea, but it still got him killed.

One of my best friends in high school went out on our graduation night and shot the windows out of the house where a black family lived. Had he not bragged and boasted about it, he would probably have gotten away with it. But because he had a big mouth, he got 10 years in the state penitentiary. Probably should have gotten more, but this was the Arkansas of the '50s and some things just were not taken too seriously.

• • •

Two years after my ride home from church with Mr. Ledbetter, he died. I was true to my word and prayed for him a lot but to my knowledge, he never got right with the Lord. I guess whatever he needed he didn't get that day when he heard me preach. That always bothered me a little bit.

• • •

Rev. Moses was beat up by a bunch of drunk redneck cowards one night when he and his family were coming home from Blytheville. He had made the mistake of not bowing his head and looking off to the side when he was asked a question by the white woman who worked the cash register at the ESSO station where he bought gas. So on the way home his car was run off the road and he was taught a lesson.

I don't think it came from the beating, but he died during my first year in college. He was my friend and my mentor. I loved that old man and he loved me. I went to his funeral with my mama and my daddy. Mr. R.C. and his wife and Bro. Earl Lee and his wife were there too. Just the seven us among a sea of black.

The funeral lasted six hours and Mr. R.C. wept harder than any person I ever saw mourn. Bro. Earl Lee probably came in second on the mourning. As far as me, I was just sad. So sad that I thought I, too, would just about die.

• • •

During those high school years I had to start thinking about college. Just the fact that this crossed my mind caused a heated discussion within the "anti-education clergy" of the area, but one particular teacher continued to urge me to go to college.

Mrs. Templeton, our English teacher, never ceased to push the issue. Before my high school days were over, she convinced me that I needed to go to college. She also had connected me to a sponsor family who would pay much of my way through college and had gotten me an academic scholarship in English that would also help pay the way.

So I was ending my high school days on a high. I had parents who loved me and supported my decisions. I had a brother who stood up for me and even took a liking to me. Sure, we still fought a lot, but we loved one another even if neither of us wanted to admit it. I had friends who allowed me to still be human and not give me a hard time about being a preacher. I had one white and one black mentor who taught me the ways of the ministry. I had a scholarship to college and a teacher who paved the way for my journey on the road out of Frostbite, Arkansas.

Yes, I had it all and I was on my way. At least I had it all except the much-talked-about call. For that, I was still listening for a voice in the night or a fire in a bush.

At that point in my life, neither had come my way.

Fourteen

It was not easy being a man of the cloth while still a sophomore in high school. For that matter, the road did not get any easier in the junior or senior years either. This was especially so if the man of the cloth being referred to was 5'5", 110 pounds of sin-leaning flesh with a doubtful calling. Such was the predicament I found myself in during that time of life. This period would not set a solid foundation for my later years and would come back to haunt my darkest dreams for years to come.

There are three things I learned during this time. First, I learned that the people who studied such things and took surveys to prove their point were absolutely correct when they announced that the number one fear in life for most people was the fear of speaking before a crowd. Some people fainted when they stood up to speak. Others were known to simply not show up at their appointed hour. Not me! My curse was to have within me that still small voice that always, I do not mean occasionally or just from time to time, but I mean that voice *always* called upon me to go to the restroom about two minutes before I was to lay the Word of the Lord on the people of God.

This usually happened about the time the person introducing me said, "We are pleased to have this here boy from Frostbite with us today to preach the Word of the Lord to us." Since that was about the extent of the introductions because I had not developed a long résumé of accomplishments at that time in my life, I usually found myself hearing that still small voice somewhere between "pleased to hear" and "today to preach to us." I must tell you this caused no small amount of embarrassment on my part. It also caused me to develop some very unique methodology to come up with a way to move from the platform where I was being introduced to the outhouse where I could satisfy the longings of the still small voice.

The most common way was to find out who prayed the longest in whatever church I might be visiting and then, immediately upon being introduced, I would call on that person to pray. Just to be safe, I would ask that person to lead us in a prayer and then provide a long list of things I thought should be covered. It had been my experience that I needed approximately three minutes to move from any church platform to a place of comfort between a couple of cars and back to the platform before the people opened their eyes.

You see, Baptists bow their heads and close their eyes when they pray. They are taught to do that from the time they are very small to the time they die. The preacher is always saying, "Now with every eye closed and with every head bowed, we are going to have Mr. Whoever lead us in prayer." So in a Baptist church, I was always safe in using this first technique. I could get the prayer started, make a dash for the door, pay my respects to the still small voice, and be back with my head being among that every-head-bowed group without anyone being the wiser.

Much later, somewhere around my senior year in high school, I was asked to deliver the morning homily at the local Episcopalian church in Blytheville. I did not know — I swear to you no one had ever told me and I did not know

— that Episcopalians *read* their prayers, thus always praying with their eyes *open.*

After enduring the longest introduction of my life, courtesy of the rector of St. James Episcopal Church in Blytheville, I called on someone to pray and dashed for the door. Three hundred pair of eyes followed my every move. One has to remember that a good Episcopalian prayer may last about 30 seconds on a good day and on that particular day, 30 seconds was not enough to complete my conversation with the still small voice within.

Upon my return, those 300 pair of eyes followed me back to the altar and, I do believe, there was a slight hint of laughter that rippled through the sanctuary.

Episcopalians call their place of worship a sanctuary. Baptist call theirs an auditorium. I asked Bro. Earl Lee what the difference was and he said that a sanctuary was just an auditorium that cost too much. I never did find out whether or not that was true, but it made sense to me.

It was after this experience at St. James Episcopal Church that word spread throughout the South that there was a boy preacher from Frostbite, Arkansas, who always had to go to the restroom about the time he was being introduced. In fact, Rev. Moses said that if I didn't get things under control I was going to have people introduce me saying, "We is pleased today to have this fine young man to preach for us. Most of you have probably heard of him. He is the one that is known as the 'pissin' preacher from Frostbite, Arkansas." Rev. Moses always knew how to build up my confidence. Unfortunately, he was also a prophet.

But anyway, my first tactic to overcome this problem was the long-winded prayer approach and that served me very well as long as I stayed among the Baptists.

The second approach I used to solve my little problem was to come straight out and lie. Immediately upon being introduced, I would turn to the music director — or song leader as they were called before they got educated and music directing became a full-time job — and say, "I am going to ask Bro. So-and-So to come and lead us in a hymn. I left a little page of notes in my car and, during this song, I am going to run and get them. I know y'all want the full load today and I don't want to short you." That always got a laugh. While they sang "Shall We Gather at the River," I was outside starting a little river of my own, if you know what I mean.

My daddy and mama always tried to go hear me any time I preached and, by now, I was preaching almost every Sunday. About the fourth time I used this second approach, my daddy nailed me pretty good on the way home. "That was a pretty good sermon today, but I'm a little worried about you, boy."

I indicated that I didn't know anything that should cause worry.

Without cracking a smile, he said, "Well, this here is the fourth time this month you forgot them notes and had to go back to the car to get 'em. Getting to be a forgetful little bastard, ain't you?"

I didn't answer. He didn't pursue the subject. I looked for another way around the problem.

My third approach was to try to not drink anything of a liquid nature from Saturday noon until after my sermon on Sunday morning. I don't know how long the human body can go without water, but 24 hours was about the limit for me. Usually by introduction time, my mouth felt like cotton and that little hangie-down thing in my throat was stuck to the roof of my mouth. Later when I got educated and didn't raise much Cain in the pulpit, that wasn't so bad. Folks just thought it was another dry sermon. But during those high school years, I was still trying to shout, preach at least an hour, and stay on rhythm like Rev. Moses had taught me. That was just plain near impossible without any water in my body.

Unfortunately, the dear sisters in the church would see that I was struggling because of a dry throat. Usually, about 15 minutes into the sermon, one would slip out and get me a nice cool glass of water and come place it on the pulpit by me. That presented me with one of two choices: I could preach on while lusting after that drink of water that was not six inches from my hand or I could just go on and drink it and immediately have to cut my sermon short by 30 minutes. This was quit a dilemma because when a bunch of Baptists are paying you $10 for a sermon, they don't what any Methodist sermonette. Very soon, I think it was after only using it on two occasions, I had to abandon this third approach.

Finally, I developed a fourth approach that worked pretty well. I learned the phrase, "The Lord laid it upon my heart." I had already learned that this simple phrase would allow any man of the cloth to get away with murder. So I just integrated it into my professional manner and it served me very well right on up to the present day.

Under this system, I would let the person introducing me do his thing, then I would walk up to the pulpit. In my simple and humble way, I would say:

Folks, the Lord is laying a special message on my heart today. And I want to make certain I am in touch with Him before we move into the sermon part of the service today. So here is what I am going to ask you to do. The Lord has laid it on my heart to go back to the back of the church and just have a quiet moment with Him before we proceed. So with every head bowed and every eye closed, I am going to ask you to pray very hard for this service. I will be back with a message from the Lord in just a few minutes. But in my short time in the Lord's service, I have learned that when the Lord is laying something on my heart, I need to be certain that I have the message clear before I proceed. Now y'all pray silently while I spend just a moment with the Lord in private.

I tell you, it worked like a charm. They got some extra prayer in. I got some time to make myself fit to preach the Word. Everything just worked wonderfully well once this fourth approach was developed. In all my years using the phrase "the Lord laid it on my heart," there was only one time it backfired on me. I remember every detail of that terrible experience.

I was preaching at the Black Oak Baptist Church, hometown of the fine singing group called Black Oak Arkansas. In the service that day was a man in his 90s with, what one might call, a whispering problem. The problem was that when he whispered, you could hear him five miles up the road. Just as I got through with my "the Lord laid it on my heart" statement and started to walk off the platform to go out back, this old gentlemen leaned over to his wife and whispered in a voice that was easily heard by everyone present, “That’s that pissin’ preacher from over at Frostbite, ain’t it?” That was a difficult moment in my rather young career, but I survived it to preach another day.

•••

Another thing I learned during those high school days was that there was a lot more about this preaching stuff than I could ever have imagined. In my naiveté, I just assumed that the entire gig consisted of preaching one or two sermons on Sunday, learning to get the connectors and rhythm down, and getting the hang of lifting the offering. Frankly, since I was preaching about every Sunday in some little country church in and around Mississippi County, Arkansas, and collecting $5 or $10 a Sunday, I thought this was pretty easy work. I remember well the day my illusion of simplicity was thrust into the reality of complexity.

Leroy, that Methodist Bishop-to-be, might have laughed a lot at my early attempts to preach the Word, but after a couple of years on the stump, he had about decided I was going to make it in the Lord’s service and proceeded to do all in his power to educate me in the ways of theology. Being well-aware of my knowledge void in the technical areas of the Lord’s work, he did realize he was facing a daunting task.

On one very hot day in July, we were sitting under the big oak tree that stood in front of the Frostbite High School for as long as anyone could remember. It had become a tradition to carve your name in the tree trunk on the night of the senior prom.

That tradition held until about 1946 when Hunk Rose came back from World War II and finished his last year of high school. On the night of the senior prom, he got drunk and took an axe and carved out about a six-inch wedge in the majestic oak and almost killed it. When arrested for the crime, he explained that his name was Hunk and all he was doing was carving his name with the axe. Being a war hero in that he didn't get shot or nothing like that, he was released into the custody of his daddy, who carved *his* name in Hunk's rear end with a boot. However, since his signature almost killed the tree, future graduates were asked to refrain from the carving ritual.

But anyway, on that particular day, Leroy and I were just sitting with our backs against the tree drinking a Coke, talking about my future.

"You doing a lot of preaching, ain't you?"

With a little bit of "I told you so" pride, I answered that I was and that it seemed the Lord was using me in a mighty way. I went on to explain that my only hang-up was that, even after all this preaching, I still had not heard the mighty voice of God calling me to preach His Holy Word.

"Well," assured Leroy, "just in case He does, you might as well keep preparing. Let me ask you this. What do you know about them sacraments?"

Not having the foggiest idea what he was talking about, I immediately locked onto the only word I understood him to say, which was *mints.* I explained that I liked them pretty good and thought it was a terrible thing you could not buy them at Mr. R.C.'s store. I also explained how good they were if you put them on ice and got them real cold before you took a bite.

When I got no response, I looked over and Leroy was just shaking his head like he was at the point of totally giving up on my ministry. Without any real malice in his voice, he just sort of whispered, "Lord, he ain't gonna make it. Lord, he is my friend but he may be dumber than a stump when it comes to things of religion."

Then after this little interlude with the Lord, he turned his attention back to me, "Buddy boy, let me tell you. If you don't get the sacraments down, you ain't never gonna get no church to have you as a preacher on a full-time basis.

"When I talk about the sacraments I ain't talking about no mints at Mr. R.C.'s store. I'm talking about baptizing folks and giving them the Lord's Supper. You dumb nitwit, do you have any idea what I am talking about?"

"Well, I guess I do! Over at our church, we do baptizing just like Jesus was baptized by dunking folks all the way under the water. We don't do none of that damp rag dripping y'all do over there at the Methodist church. And another thing, we do the Lord's Supper once every three months just like the 14 disciples did it in the Bible."

"It was 12!"

"What?"

"It was 12 disciples. Lord, Sam don't you ever read the Bible? Or do you just get up there and rhyme and shout?" I could tell he was pretty frustrated so I just kept my mouth shut, which was probably the only thing I did right that entire day.

For about the next hour, Leroy quizzed me on the ins and outs of baptism and communion and other such holy acts — and in most cases I failed. So since it was hot anyway and since the Baptist church always kept the baptistery full of water, he decided we ought to go over to the Baptist church and do a little practicing.

As usual, the church was unlocked so we proceeded to go up into the choir loft and looked over the top of the glass at the water.

"Test it."

"What do you mean, test it?"

"Put your hand in the water and see if it's cold 'cause if it is, I ain't gonna let you do no practicing on me," replied Leroy, and he said it like he really meant it.

I stood up on one of the folding chairs in the choir loft, reached over the glass, and stuck my hand in the water. It felt pretty good, but about this time it was dawning on me what Leroy had in mind. He was going to have me practice my baptizing skills on him right there at that very moment. I was surprised, but since I needed the practice, and I figured a little Baptist dunking wouldn't hurt my good Methodist friend. I proclaimed the water to be at an acceptable temperature.

Leroy then explained what we were going to do. "Okay, now we are going to the back of the church to the stairs going up into the baptistery and you are going to practice baptizing me. Now here is the way it goes."

"Leroy, we ain't got no swimming suits with us. My mama will kill me if I get these fresh-ironed jeans wet. So how we gonna do this?"

Obviously he had already thought it through, "Does it look like there is anyone else in this church?"

I declared that it looked pretty empty to me.

"Well, what we are gonna do is get up there and take our clothes off and do some skinny baptizing just like we do skinny dipping down at Morgan's Creek. Good thing is that, up here in the baptistery, we won't have to worry about no water moccasins. Now if you will get on with it, we can be out of here in about 15 minutes, but you got to get this baptizing down. Now shut up and come on!"

That seemed like a pretty good answer to me so I proceeded to follow Leroy into the back of the church where we could have access to the baptistery. All the way back he was telling me the exact words I was to say and giving me tips on the timing of the dunking.

"What we do is both stand looking at the side wall so the congregation is looking at our sides. You will be right behind me and you will say something like this. 'We are proud to have our brother, Leroy, here tonight to proclaim his faith in Jesus. So I am going to baptize him.' At that point you will raise your right hand in the air and put your other hand on my chest. Then you will say, 'I baptize you my brother in the name of the Father and the Son and the Holy Ghost.'

"Now the minute you say 'I baptize you,' you will dunk me under the water and will hold me there until you finish repeating the rest of the sentence about the Father, Son and Holy Ghost. You got that?"

Since it didn't seem too hard to me, I assured him that I had it down and up the stairs we went into the baptistery loading zone or whatever you call it. Like two kids at the swimming hole on a hot summer day, we stripped our clothes off and got in the baptistery.

The first time I tried to baptize Leroy I got him under the water okay, but I couldn't remember the words and while I was trying to think about them, I almost drowned him. If he hadn't got his free hand around my neck and jerked himself out of the water, I guess I would have probably been practicing for my first funeral.

The second time I remembered the words just like he had told me, but we got off balance and his feet came up out of the water just as his head went under thus nullifying the term of total immersion. Leroy was getting a little upset.

Just as we started for the third try, Aunt Mamie Sullivan opened the door of the auditorium, threw on all the lights, and walked in with about 10 of her G.A. (Girl's Auxiliary) teenage girls. If you are not of the Baptist persuasion, what you might not know is that the front to the baptistery facing the congregation is made of glass so that the whole congregation can be assured the preacher fully dunks the newborn Christian. It was that glass that I was reaching over while standing on the folding chair in the choir loft a few minutes earlier.

So just as Aunt Mamie hit the light switch, Leroy and I turned in our total nakedness to face 11 pair of very wide eyes belonging to Aunt Mamie and the girls from the Baptist church G.A. division. I do not know the exact time, but somewhere in the range of 10 seconds several things happened. Aunt Mamie hit the light switch thus turning off the lights, 10 young ladies were introduced to the minister and his first baptismal candidate in a way they would never forget, and Leroy and I almost drowned each other getting back to our clothes.

I think it was the next day that Leroy passed me a note in Algebra class. Printed in very small print, it read, "I ain't even gonna dare try to teach you nothing about the Lord's Supper. My teaching days are over, boy. You are on your own!"

• • •

Finally, the third thing I learned during those high school days was that a bad day of preaching was better than a good day chopping cotton any day. My daddy had acres of cotton on his farm. One of the rituals of summer was to chop the weeds out of the cotton rows. It was hot, back-breaking work and everyone in the family was obliged to do his part.

I remember one day in my sophomore year in high school when I was working in the field just trying to make the day go faster. The sun was hotter than a three-dollar bill and there was not a cloud in the sky or a breeze in the air. It was hot. All those pictures you have seen of the slaves chopping or picking cotton while they sang old gospel hymns were a bunch of baloney. That is hot, dirty work, and in all my growing-up years in the fields, I never once heard no heavenly music.

About three that afternoon, as we were coming to the end of about a half-mile row, I looked up to see Bro. Earl Lee and the evangelist, who was preaching the summer revival at our church, driving up in a new Oldsmobile. It seems the evangelist had a pretty good run through the spring and the lifting of the offerings had been productive. So Bro. Earl Lee's mode of transportation had jumped up a notch. That car looked like a million dollars and, as they got closer, I noticed the windows were rolled up. That thing was air-conditioned!

When they stopped, Bro. Earl Lee rolled down his window about halfway and sort of yelled out to all us field hands as we were called, "Just wanted to stop by and invite all y'all to church tonight. The reverend here is going to be preaching on heaven and I know y'all gonna want to come." Not waiting for an answer, he rolled up the window and they slowly pulled off on down the road with a cloud of Mississippi County dust rolling up behind them.

While we stood there in the 105-degree heat just watching them disappear, Danny leaned over toward me and said in my ear, "Boy, you feeling called yet? If you ain't, then something must be wrong with your calling mechanism."

It could have been my imagination, but I do faintly remember hearing a voice in my soul saying, "Go preach, boy. Go preach." It was faint, no doubt about that, but I do believe I remember it.

Fifteen

To be a "preacher boy" in a small country church was about the top of the social pecking order when we were in high school. In my class of 13 students, there were two of us who were destined for the ministry. Leroy, the one called by the voice of a Methodist God who didn't seem to provide Leroy with any preaching opportunities, and the one nailed by the church elders. We both gave all we had to honor the calling in whatever manner it had been presented.

We were given no training in sermon preparation. No introduction to the Bible was forthcoming. If we did not have all we needed after 12 or 13 years in Sunday school, then all the training in the world was not going to help. So we were just sent out to do the best we could with what we had discovered along life's way.

And the amazing thing about it was, people actually invited me to preach! They acted as though they were blessed by my words and, very often, invited me home to eat a fine Sunday dinner with their family. Looking back on it, that wasn't all bad.

Leroy, while never actually becoming a pastor of a church, did become a chaplain in the United States of America Army.

From that time in high school all the way through my seminary years, I heard a lot of would-be preachers proclaim the Word. But I must tell you, I am somewhat partial to those whose first sermon was under a tree somewhere as opposed to one whose first sermon was in a seminary class.

When I was in seminary, our preaching professor, Dr. Samuel Woodson, was a great theologian. His books provided the outline for many a student's early sermons. And when he complimented you, it was as though the voice of God had spoken. And when he criticized you, your only hope was that somehow you might someday get a job as a church janitor.

In his class, each student was required to prepare a sermon and preach it to the class. It was put on video, old Sony beta if I remember correctly, and played back to the class while the good professor critiqued the content and delivery.

One of my classmates worked all semester on his sermon. We sat in my apartment while he practiced on me. His outline was a masterpiece and every word was carefully chosen to make just the right impact. He was 22 years old, graduated from a major Baptist university, had two years of seminary behind him, and had *never* preached a sermon in his life. On the day of his sermon before the class, he crashed and burned.

The moment he stood behind the pulpit in our preaching class, everyone knew he was in trouble. I had visions of my own five-minute wonder, preached in that little church in Frostbite, Arkansas. He forgot every word, could not read his notes, and had no idea how to ad lib. He breezed through his 25 minutes of allotted time in six short and very miserable minutes.

Dr. Woodson spent about two minutes trying to comfort the poor soul before failing him in the class, thus delaying his graduation by another full semester. Then he looked straight at me and said, "Mr. Hamilton, I know you are not scheduled to preach until next Monday, but if you are ready now, we would be pleased to hear from you."

As in most of my classes, I was totally unprepared. I had planned to spend the weekend preparing for my class sermon. But when Dr. Woodson called, one was not wise to turn a deaf ear. So with no hesitation, I got up from my chair and, with my Bible in hand, went to the pulpit. For the next 25 minutes, I preached a sermon that had been heard all over the Mississippi Delta country during my high school days.

I used the experiences of my youth and combined them with the lessons of the semester to preach the message of Christ with power and persuasion. You see, this was not my first time to be called on short notice. Many of my high school assignments came about because some country preacher had gotten up on Sunday morning with a sore throat and needed a quick substitute. By the time Dr. Woodson called on me, I had probably preached 50 or so extemporaneous sermons. This was nothing new to me.

I was watching the clock and I knew that Dr. Woodson needed about 10 minutes at the end of the sermon to critique my presentation before the class. So I brought my sermon to a close at exactly 10 minutes before the sound of the bell. As I walked down from the pulpit to go back to my seat, I noticed that Dr. Woodson was not moving toward the front of the class as he usually did after the student sermon. He was just sitting in one of the chairs with his head down.

Minutes passed. Not a word was spoken. I did not know whether I had passed or failed. We had never seen him wait even one minute before making his comments. I was married with one child, working three jobs, and going to school full-time. I could not afford to fail this class and yet, the man just sat there. The minutes dragged on, one by one. We were getting closer and closer to the end of the class and still, he had not moved.

Then finally, with perfect timing, he arose from his seat and turned to the class. There were tears in his eyes. In almost a whisper he said to me, in front of my classmates, "Mr. Hamilton, today you blessed my heart. May God bless you for sharing that with us." And with that, the bell rang and we went to our next class.

In the years ahead, I would cling to that comment a thousand times when I fought the battles that come with the pastoral territory.

• • •

About five years later, I was on a national program as a speaker and was surprised to learn that Dr. Woodson would also be a speaker at the conference.

When we met that time, we were no longer student and professor. We were co-laborers for the Kingdom.

After one of the sessions, we met in the hotel coffee shop and shared a few moments of fellowship. He recalled the experience in his class that day I got up and preached. He shared with me that, at that time, he and his family were going through a great trial. Though he did not say what it was, I could look in his eyes and see that the memory was still sensitive to his soul. As we sat there, he said, "You know what you said that day was not profound. I recognized your sermon as only one country boy can recognize another. As I heard you speak that day, I renewed my commitment to God that had been made in a little country church in Mississippi long years before. My soul was ready for what you said, and God used it in a mighty way."

I sat there humbled by his words. Suddenly it was becoming clear that the vessel might not have been formed for the task, but God was able to use it to hold holy water. I did not share my still-unresolved doubts with my old professor that night. But I returned to my room with a renewed prayer that I might someday hear the call of God to be such a vessel in His service.

Sixteen

But I digress and get ahead of my story. I was to preach many a bad sermon before finally reaching the hallowed halls of a great seminary. First, I had to go to college and get the education that Mrs. Templeton had insisted I complete before going out to save the world.

About the time I announced that I was going off to college, I received another visit from the Elders. This time there was no surprise to it. They just called and asked if they could come visit with my mama, my daddy, and me on one Sunday afternoon. Being that I was about the most famous boy preacher in Mississippi County, Arkansas, I felt pretty honored to give them an audience.

It was a trick! They came to our house that Sunday afternoon not to praise me for the good preaching I was doing, but to try to stop the college train from pulling out of town.

Bro. Earl Lee led the conversation, "Bro. Elroy, the word is out that the boy is a leaving here to go off to some college up north. Reckon you could fill us in on that little plan of his?"

I could tell right then by the look in his eyes that my daddy did not like the way this conversation was beginning. "Well, I guess Sam can speak for his self so why don't you talk to him? Looks to me like he is sittin' about as close to you and I am, so just ask him."

Daddy had about quit calling me "boy" and was more and more using my real name. He was a little perturbed that Bro. Earl Lee and everyone else in town hadn't made the change right along with him. So right from the start, Bro. Earl Lee got on my daddy's bad side. You could tell by the sort of frosty chill in his voice when he directed Bro. Earl Lee to talk directly to me.

However, with no visible signs of sensitivity growing within the heart of Bro. Earl Lee, he just turned to me and charged on down the road. "Well, boy, what about it? You think you got to go off to one of them Yankee schools to learn how to preach? Looks like to me you been racking it in pretty good with just the education you got from the fine teachers at Frostbite High School. That ain't good enough for you?"

This boy had some explaining to do. "No, sir, it ain't that. It just seems like if I'm gonna preach the Word, then I ought to at least go somewhere I can learn things like they was 12 disciples, not 14, and that it was Jonah and the whale and not Noah and the whale, and some of that detailed stuff."

Then I looked at the Elders and you could see I had hit a pretty good note with them because all over the county it was known that I might be loud, but I was not always accurate. I saw a few grins among the group.

But Bro. Earl Lee took offense and continued his attack, "Well, well, well. Looks like I ain't educated enough to guide you in the ministry of the Lord. Looks like you looking for a little more than this poor country preacher can give you, don't it? Well, let me tell you something, boy. You gonna go off to one of them college places and they gonna fill your head with all that liberal stuff, and the Lord only knows what you will be preaching two or three years from now."

"It's four years, Earl Lee," everyone turned to hear what my mama had said under her breath.

"What's that, Martha? You say something?"

"Yes, I did Earl Lee. I said it takes four years to go to college, not two or three. And there's a few other things I want to say." I looked at my daddy and I could tell he knew Bro. Earl Lee was in for it. Just the look in Mama's eyes indicated that she was about to light into him, and Daddy and I figured we better just keep our mouths shut.

"I want to say that I think it is time you stopped calling my son 'boy' and started using his real name. Earl Lee, his name is Sam after Samuel in the Bible. You don't call Samuel in the Bible 'boy,' do you?" She was in no mood to wait for an answer.

"I been thinking about this for three years, ever since Sam preached down at the colored church. Seems like ever since that time you sort of been on his back about something. You always trying to act kind and helpful, but you seem to put him down every time he preaches for us at our church. No wonder Sam likes preaching in Moses' church better than over at ours. Moses, God bless his black soul, has done more for Sam than you ever did, and I think it is time you own up to it. You understand me?"

"Now, Martha slow ..."

"Don't you tell me to slow down. I ain't near through with you. My son has a chance to go to college, and he is gonna go if I have to push him there in a wheelbarrow. They ain't a one of us in this room that ever got to go to college, and he has his chance and he is gonna take it.

"And another thing. He ain't going to no Yankee school, he is going down to Texas. So you might want to get that straight while you're at it.

"And with the good Lord's help, it may be that he will find out who called him to preach. I think in his mind right now he don't know whether it was you and this bunch of elders or if it was the Lord, and it is about time he finds out."

"No, Martha, you know we got the Word of the ..."

Mama was not to be stopped, "Don't tell me you got the Word of the Lord telling you my Sam was to be a preacher. You did that to his real daddy, God rest his soul, and I ain't gonna stand by and watch you do it to him. Sam is going off to college, and every day I am gonna pray he finds his way. If God has called him to preach, I reckon he will be smart enough to hear the voice of God his self. And if he don't hear the Lord calling, at least he will be far enough away from here that he won't have to listen to you tell him he has been called and then put him down every time he tries to do what you say he ought to be doing.

"Now, Earl Lee, since you seem to be speaking for the group here, you got anything else to say?" Everybody in the room knew she was not looking for an answer to that question, but Bro. Earl Lee had a way of not listening to what was actually being said so he plunged right in.

"Well, I think what we came over here to do has about been done. We just wanted to tell the boy — excuse me, we wanted to tell Sam that he was gonna face some fierce evil out in the real world and that we are gonna be praying for him. Ain't that right, fellows?" Heads moved up and down vigorously letting everyone in the room know that Mama had at least gotten through to them with her mighty speech.

"So I guess we better be going. Sam, if you don't mind, let's get on our knees and ask the Lord to take care of you and bring you back with the same stuff in your head that you leave with. That all right, Martha?"

Mama looked him straight in the eye, "Earl Lee, you be careful what you pray for, but go ahead and say one. Sam is gonna need it, and it will help me get a feel of what you are gonna be praying about. So go ahead on."

As was the custom, we all got on our knees there in the living room and Bro. Earl Lee cut loose. He got all the preliminaries out of the way, and then got to the points he had really come to make had it not been for Mama's frontal attack on him. "Lord, you know Sam is on his way to get educated ... or so he thinks. Well, don't let them liberal commie professors get him off the beaten track ... like we know they will. Get him back here as quick as possible so's we can guide him back to the way of the Lord. Thank you, Jesus. Now we all say Amen."

We had not yet made it back to our sitting up position when Mama just had to get in one more word, "Well, Earl Lee, if that is gonna be the direction of your praying for Sam, you might want to just keep it to yourself. God's got big things for my son and I got me a feeling that they are not going to be found if he comes back here to Frostbite.

"Now, can I offer all y'all some coffee and chocolate pie? Just made it fresh this morning."

Everyone agreed that they did have time for a piece of Mama's famous chocolate pie and coffee, and so we sat down and had a fine time together around the big round table in Mama's kitchen. The serious stuff was all out of the way. Now we were just a bunch of neighbors having a good time talking about things in general. Everyone had said their peace, and everyone had listened whether they agreed or not.

That was the way it was in Frostbite on the last day before I would get on the bus and leave there forever. I would leave a way of life that had been a pretty good ride, but somewhere at the end of the bus line, I sure hoped it was gonna get better. Little did I know what was out there.

Seventeen

By now, it was almost four in the afternoon and I had been sitting under this old willow tree for about two hours. The memories were taking me back to places I had not been in what seemed like a hundred years. It had been pretty hot, but as it hit mid-afternoon, a slight wind picked up and it was not stifling like it had been.

I decided to check in with Sarah. She answered her cell phone immediately and we talked for a minute. She was on a slow baby-picture tour of my childhood and made comments to describe the situation. I could tell that my bare bottom was going to be framed on the piano as soon as we went home. It was fun to hear her version of the afternoon.

Just about the time I started to fill her in on my afternoon out here under the tree, Gary Lynn Houston drove up. I said a quick good-bye and "I'll meet you back at the church around six" just as Gary Lynn parked his truck and got out.

Waving in that back-hand casual way of the Delta, he strolled over to where I was sitting, ducking his head to move under the long sleepy branches of the willow.

I had not seen Gary Lynn since my days in Frostbite. Shirley, his sister, and I broke up, and since Gary Lynn was a couple of years younger than my buddies, we had just drifted apart. He was at the service that morning honoring

Mama, but had slipped out before I had a chance to say hello.

"Hope you don't mind me barging into your treehouse here, but I saw Sarah and she told me you were out here." He looked around, then dropped down on the ground beside me. He had a casual way about him that felt easy on this slow afternoon.

He waited a minute then said, "Things changed a lot since you were here last. Looks as if the old house is about gone."

"Yea, a lot of water has gone under the bridge since we played ball out here after school."

There was a pause, a long pause in the way that seemed natural to Delta people. Then the conversation moved on as though we had not been separated by a lifetime. It seemed as if he was waiting for me to close the years in between, so I just said the first thing that came to mind. "I hear Shirley moved to Memphis and married some big-time lawyer. I sure thought I was going to be your brother-in-law around the ninth grade."

"Yea, and I thought I was gonna have a preacher in the family. You probably don't know, no reason for you to, but Shirley got breast cancer a couple of years ago and she is pretty much at the end right now. They gave her all that shit, but it didn't seem to help. Probably another month or two."

"Oh man, Gary Lynn, I hadn't heard. I'm so sorry."

"Yea, she and Jim have three kids, all grown with families now, but it's gonna be a tough time on everyone. God, that woman has suffered.

"By the way," he said seeming to want to change the subject. "I stopped being 'Gary Lynn' a long time ago. Most folks started calling me Gary after I hit 40."

We laughed in an old friend, casual way when I replied, "Yea, and so far today no one has called me 'boy.'"

About that time, the second truck of the day passed down the road. The driver looked to be about 16 and was driving about 70 miles an hour on that gravel road. Thank goodness the wind was blowing the opposite way or we would have been covered in Delta dust.

"That was Harry Rogers' boy. Think they moved here after you left. Sum-bitch is gonna be dead before he's 20. Already totaled Harry's new car last year. Seems like we got out about the right time, Sam. Worse thing we ever did was steal a few watermelons. Now they shoot up stuff, drive like hell, and get every girl in the county pregnant."

I agreed that things had changed. Another long pause. The wind picked up a bit and the hawk was back in the air. No one spoke for a while.

Then Gary Lynn started, "Sam, can I ask you a personal question? None of my business, but when did you decide to stop preaching? Damn, you were good at it. What happened?"

"Things just took a turn like they do sometimes. Maybe it was going off to college, seeing the world from a different perspective than the Rev. Earl Lee version. I don't know."

"Old Earl Lee. That man was something wasn't he? I think the only time I ever figured out he had a heart and wasn't secretly wishing us all into hell was when old Moses died. I didn't go to the funeral, but I heard tell he cried like a baby at that old black preacher's funeral. Crazy thing was, he would have hung him from the nearest tree if Moses got out of line. But when old Moses died, Bro. Earl Lee seemed to take it real hard."

I wanted to say that at least there were a few of us that took it real hard when those rednecks beat him to a pulp on the side of the road but decided that Gary Lynn probably hadn't been involved, so I let it pass.

"You know, it's sort of funny now, but I had a pretty rough time when I heard you stopped preaching. Man, did I look up to you. Wanted to be just like you. I went to Arkansas State, got a degree in education. In fact, I went on to get my Doctor's degree in history and have been teaching over at State for almost 20 years now.

"You would be surprised at how I developed my lectures at first. I used your mannerisms, tried to be dramatic like you were when you preached. I guarantee you one thing, when they got out of History 101, they knew they had heard some Southern preaching mixed in with it. That came from you. Okay, *boy,* so what happened?"

We both chuckled with the reference to my former name. Then the wind stirred the willow. The hawk landed on a fencepost and almost immediately took flight again. It flew in wide circles above the cotton field across the road. I followed it with my eyes while trying to think with my heart how to answer Gary Lynn's question.

Eighteen

THE NEXT DAY, MY SUITCASE was packed and we all got in the pickup to drive me to the bus station in Blytheville. Things were pretty quiet on the drive to town. I was the first to leave home, and I think my Mama looked a little older for it. Daddy usually hummed or whistled on the drive, but today things were pretty quiet.

My bus was to leave for Memphis at 11:05 that morning and being punctual as always, Daddy had us in the truck by nine. After all, it would take about 30 minutes to make the drive, thus giving us a full hour and a half to stand around and try to think of something to say.

The bus station had been built a few years before and was that Greyhound art-deco style that most of us just thought looked pretty goofy. On this day in 1957, it was just another bus stop with a few people waiting to get out of this Godforsaken county. There were four of us waiting: three of us in the white waiting room and one over in the colored.

Every few minutes, Mama would reach over and rub my head like she had for as long as I could remember. She could say more with that touch than some people could say talking for an hour. My brother, that sorry miserable piece of humanity, was off to seeing some girl over on Ash Street, so as least he was out of the way.

Finally, about 15 minutes before the bus came, my daddy looked over at me and suggested we go for a walk. We went out behind the station; he lit up a smoke and kind of rubbed his left shin with his right boot. I could tell he wanted to say something so I just let it ride until he was ready. Finally he found some words, "Sam, it ain't gonna be the same around here without you. You write your mama, you hear?"

I promised I would, but didn't add anything else. I guess if the truth were told, I was fighting a lump in my own throat about that time.

He cleared his throat and finally got to the point, "We gonna miss you, boy. Ain't no lying about that, we are gonna miss you. But I want you to know I'm mighty proud of you. Not everyone from Frostbite is catching a bus today to go off to college. You know what I mean?"

I allowed that I did and admitted to myself that this was probably the longest serious talk we had ever had. Daddy usually left the talking to Mama. He continued, "Well, I know you got them nice folks helping pay your way and I know Mrs. Templeton has helped you get a job, so you probably not gonna need much. At the same time, I want to do what I can. So take this and use it when you need it. I'll be sending more if I can save it up."

He reached in his pocket and pulled out a hundred dollar bill and stuffed it in my shirt. He was right. It wouldn't go far, but he was also right when he said he would send me more. For the next four years, Daddy sent me a five or a ten about every month and I knew it was hard saved.

The now-shortened cigarette was thrown on the ground and the talk was over. I wanted to thank him and knew if I did we would both be crying, which was not the way for men of the Delta. So I just nodded my head and followed him back inside. The bus would come in about five minutes and this boy from Frostbite, with a beat-up old suitcase that my uncle had given me and a crisp new hundred-dollar bill, would be on it.

Life was about to change more than I knew.

Nineteen

BEING A GOOD BAPTIST BOY, I CHOSE a fine Baptist school almost a thousand miles from home. I figured that was about as good as it could get.

Two days after leaving Frostbite, I was in the middle of the Texas heat, sitting in a dorm room with my new roommate whose daddy was the current governor of Texas. I think we each served as an oddity for the other, but we got along pretty good. He was astounded by my history and his money astounded me. So much so that three years later, when I got married, I would hock my FM radio over to him for a $200 loan to buy an engagement ring. I paid it back in three months so we were square.

I knew I was in the right place when, after unpacking, he looked over at me and said, "Well, boy, let's go case this joint." It had the feel of home about it.

My first English class had more people in it than the total population of Frostbite. The university had more than 10,000 students — more than the population of Blytheville that was, up until that time, the biggest town I ever spent any time in. But the worst part was, this "preaching wonder" had no place to preach.

Sunday after Sunday came and went and not one invitation came. So this was what being educated was all about? You got to learn a lot, but it didn't seem to go for much good.

About midway through my second semester, my student advisor asked me if I would like to be considered to pastor a little country church out from Dawson, Texas. I jumped at the idea. About three weeks later I was pastor of my first church of 11 members and, as far as I know, one family of five who were the only prospects. Bless their old lost souls, that family got a visit from me every Sunday until, finally, two of them got saved and joined the church. Since that was the first baptism in the church in 17 years, it was a pretty big deal. Not every first-year preacher boy increased his church's membership by almost 20 percent in the first three months of his tenure.

Every Sunday I would get in the old $350-car I bought and drive the 60 miles to Dawson, hit the dirt road, then drive another 10 miles and preach the Word of the Lord. But success was fast fleeting. My fifth month there, the only deacon died on a Monday. When I went down on the following Sunday, there was a committee of three waiting to see me, questioning why I did not come down to comfort the family. When I explained that no one called me, I was told that there were just some things you were supposed to know it you were a Man of God. They didn't ask me to resign, but I thought about it anyway. I didn't. The next Sunday we had seven people in church. Seemed to me things were not going too well.

At the start of my junior year, I was asked to become the pastor of another church that was about 90 miles south of the university. It had about 50 members and had always had preacher "boys" as pastor. I jumped at the chance. I drove off every Sunday morning around 5 AM to make the drive down for the morning service. The afternoon would be spent visiting around or playing baseball with some boys not much younger than I was. I would then preach again that night, then take my old '53 Studebaker, usually loaded with watermelons or fresh meat, back to campus. I got paid $10 a week and that almost paid for my gas.

By that time I met Sarah and she started going with me on Sunday. She could play the piano, which was good because the only other person who could play was 93-year-old Miss Selma Williams, and she could only play with three fingers on each hand because of her arthritis. One Sunday Sarah and I went to Miss Williams' home to have lunch with her. We had the monthly business meeting that morning after church and things did not go very well. Someone was mad about something and, being good Baptists, we argued about it for over an hour.

That day at lunch Miss Williams said, "You know, Bro. Sam, I sure hate to see these little country churches passing off the scene, don't you?"

I indicated that I too felt the loss, but then made the mistake of saying, "But what made you think about that today, Miss Williams?"

Without looking up from her fried chicken, mashed potatoes or fried okra, she replied, "Well, I guess I was just wondering where you boys are going to make your mistakes when there are no longer any country churches for you to practice on." Obviously, my ministerial career was not progressing as smoothly as I hoped.

College became a blur in time as the years passed in their meaningless monotony. I hated chemistry and French. I saw no relevance to Texas history and constitutional law. I just wanted to take courses in religion and learn all those things I did not know about when my preaching career started back in Frostbite.

Toward the end of our junior year, Sarah and I got married and moved into the married dorm where our concrete block bookcase looked just like everyone else's concrete block bookcase. We saved enough money for a trip back to Frostbite in our senior year. She had never met my folks and I had not returned home since leaving for college. Mama was older. Daddy was quieter. My brother, who had actually grown up to be a pretty nice guy, had gone into the Air Force and was slapping grease on A-4's flying somewhere in Southeast Asia.

My preaching career was in full force as I packed them in every Sunday. (At least I packed about 50 people in when it wasn't raining or deer season wasn't in full force.) I buried a few, married even fewer. As far as I know, no one got saved, sanctified, or set apart during my ministerial career at that second country church, but to my knowledge, none of the flock ever totally backslid into hell thus testing the Baptist belief of "once saved, always saved." I reckon once you added the two churches together, things were not really so bad.

All in all it was a pretty good four years.

We went back to Frostbite during the summer between college and seminary. Sarah was going to get her law degree, and I was going to try and finish the three-year seminary degree at the same time, so we knew that this might be our last chance to visit my family for a couple of years. Her parents lived in Dallas, so we saw them quite a bit. They were good people who seemed to enjoy hearing my accent without making fun of it.

The drive from Texas to Mississippi County, Arkansas, took a full day so we went up on Friday and had a nice visit on Saturday. Sunday was the return trip home. They asked me to preach on Sunday, but both Sarah and I had registration on Monday, so we did not want to leave after the service and then have to drive all night.

Bro. Earl Lee was still preaching and said that if I couldn't stay over, he would just plan to preach on hell in my honor. I think he was joking, but Mama wrote the next week that he had preached on hell and that she wasn't sure it "honored anyone."

Mama was getting a little testy about Bro. Earl Lee.

Twenty

IF COLLEGE HAD BEEN LIKE a sentence in hell, seminary was like a walk through a Delta cotton field after a spring rain. Every course was relevant to the cause, and I basked in the wisdom of great men of God who taught them. I was intrigued by the sacrifices of the saints and challenged by the moral crises of our time.

By this time, we were getting slaughtered in Vietnam. Mama called to tell me that Leroy had been killed in somewhere in a jungle there. Chaplains were not supposed to get killed, but he did and my heart was broken. The streets of Birmingham and Detroit were filled with the fires of racial tension. National leaders were being gunned down as though we were living in a third-world nation. It was a crazy time to be preparing for the ministry. One great preacher in the South had "a dream" and they blew his head off for it, and *this* simple preacher from the South was struggling through seminary trying to make sense of it all. And in the struggle, my mind was blown away also, but in a much less traumatic way.

And there was always the question of the call. In ethics class, someone would ask about moral relevance and the professor would say, "We always have the Word, but we also have the inner comfort of our call."

In missions class, semester after semester, great missionaries of the faith would come before us and tell of their struggles in some jungle in South America or some mud hut church in Africa and then say, "And there are times that the only thing keeping me there is the fact that I have the assurance of my call."

I had no idea what they meant! By now, I was the pastor of a somewhat larger congregation that even provided a house for Sarah and me, but I had no idea why I was there. Where was this call? Where was this assurance of vocation? Where was this great desire to save the world? Where? Where? Where? Dear God, Bro. Earl Lee! Dear, God, you damn Elders! Where is the call? Where is the voice you heard on my behalf? Where is the bush you saw burning for me? Where? I demand to know where!

Nothing changed.

Between our second and third year in graduate school, Sarah and I had our first child. Josh was born on July 16, 1964, and became the center of our life. We arranged our schedules so that one of us was always either home or able to take Josh with us to study or to the store or wherever else we needed to go.

Oh, Josh! Ten little fingers and ten tiny toes. Hair as red as a Washington apple and a smile that could melt all the tension in our lives.

I was working two jobs, pastor of another church, going to school full-time, and looking forward to the day when all this would be past and we could get on with life. Sarah was in law school and studied every night past midnight.

We worked hard, but we loved one another. Josh was the cement that held us together during that frantic time. Finally, on May 23, 1965, Sarah and I were graduated on the same day. You might know we would miss sharing the big joint event we had so looked forward to sharing.

Sarah's mother and father went to her ceremony and took care of Josh. I went to mine alone, but had a phone call from Mama about 6 AM that same morning. In the seven years I was away from home this was only the second time she called me. She thought nothing of calling so early. She was a morning person and just assumed I would be wide awake and waiting for her call. I was.

She told me how proud she was of me and how happy she was that God had called me into the ministry. She wanted me to be as good a man as Bro. Earl Lee (so I suppose he was on her good side at that time). Daddy got on the phone and mumbled something about me not getting stuck up about having all "them degrees. Makes it sound like you got the flu or something." He meant it to be funny. Maybe it was.

My graduation wasn't until 10 o'clock that morning so I read the paper, wishing Sarah and Josh didn't have to leave at 8 to go pick up her parents over in Dallas to bring them to her graduation. Her father recently had a stroke and still couldn't drive. Her mother never learned how.

So after they left, I cleaned up the house a little bit. Got out one of my two suits and decided that it was a good thing that pink and black were no longer the popular colors because I looked a lot better dressed in the blue suit in my closet. With shiny shoes and starch in my shirt, I walked across campus to get the official document that would say I had completed my degree to become a minister of the Gospel. I felt no particular sense of accomplishment. I could raise hell in the pulpit with or without a degree.

Unfortunately, I was also learning that if I hit the right note, emphasized the right verse and manipulated the right phrase, I could get them down the aisle just like Bro. Earl Lee. I had learned well and now, legally, I was becoming my "brother's" elder.

Twenty-one

JOSH DIED THAT NIGHT. I DON'T mean sometime after our great day, I mean that night. We had made it through our ceremonies, had an early dinner with Sarah's folks and a couple of close friends, then went home for our private celebration.

Suddenly, for all practical purposes, we were out of work. Our church was accustomed to "preacher boys" moving on to bigger and better things, so it was time for me to start looking for a full-time position. Sarah now had to pass the bar, which would take a few months, and then we would decide on her career path.

But we were young. And our seven years of educational hell was over. And we were in love. And Josh was the center of our little world. And there was a room in our house that we called the family room and that is what we were. That is what we had. We had each other and, wherever we went or wherever God took us, we would be just fine because we had in our home a family room.

But Josh died.

About midnight, Sarah went into his room to just make certain things were all right with him. But things were not all right. He wasn't breathing. We rushed to the emergency room. We ran every red light on the way. We screamed at the nurse to do something. The doctor came and held our hands. But Josh was still dead. His little fingers were cold and his tiny toes were blue and someone suggested we might call someone and let them know. But we went home that night alone and we cried as we spent our first night of the rest of our lives.

Later the doctors said there was a heart valve imperfection. We could not have prevented it. They could not have cured it. So Josh died.

Things changed after that. Not between Sarah and me, but just between our dreams and us. Most of the summer was spent praying that someone would recommend me to a church somewhere. Sarah continued to study for the bar. We didn't talk very much or very often, and when we did, we sometimes said too much.

Bro. Earl Lee called me and told me there was a church in Jonesboro, Arkansas, that needed a pastor and would like to hear me preach. We made plans to go up.

On a hot weekend in August, we made our way back to my starting gate. They had a good turnout for the service, about 500 people if memory serves me right. Six folks got saved that morning and about 14 rededicated their lives as Baptists are known to do from time to time.

As was the custom, after I had preached for them that day, Sarah and I met with the pulpit committee to discuss our coming to minister to them.

The first question sealed my fate with them. It came from the chairperson of the committee. I think he was a local doctor. "How do you feel about niggers coming to white churches?"

My God, it had not changed. I responded with a socially unacceptable answer, and then preached a little bit to make my point. The questions were over pretty quickly. They thanked us, and we left there to drive the 50 miles back to Mama and Daddy's house.

"I'll dig ditches for the rest of my life before I'll come back here to pastor a church."

"Well, buy me a shovel and I'll dig too," Sarah replied.

We both kind of laughed through our tears and disappointment, but it was the closest we had been to each other in a long time. I wanted that drive to last longer than it did.

•••

When we got back home, the next week I had a letter waiting for me at the seminary placement office. A bigger church — brick no less, with a larger membership in a county seat town in Texas — wanted me to come interview for a position as the senior pastor. For the first year out of seminary, there could not have been a better position. Maybe God just wanted to see if we really would go buy shovels to keep me from having to preach something I didn't believe.

For whatever the reason, six weeks later, we moved into a fine brick parsonage at the First Baptist Church in Powderville, Texas. It was our first full-time position. Eleven months later, the twins were born.

Over the next five years, we relocated the church to a new and more prominent acreage in town, the congregation tripled in size, the people loved us, and I preached the Word. Sarah found a job in the county attorney's office.

Everything looked so solid. We just seemed to have it so under control. Until one night, we had a baptismal service and I baptized 32 people into the church.

And on that night, I went home and kissed the twins good-night, and held Sarah a few minutes until she fell fast asleep. And then quietly in the night, I went into the den and took out my shot gun, put two shells in, sat down in my chair, put the barrel in my mouth, and debated blowing my brains out.

After years of preaching without the call and after learning that, with the right words, I could manipulate them down the aisles, I had just hit the bottom of my spiritual barrel. I just entered what St. John of the Cross had written about in the mid-sixteenth century, "The Dark Night of the Soul."

I did not know it would last for almost 25 years.

Twenty-two

THE HAWK CIRCLED IN AN EVER-tightening vortex until, sighting its prey between the rows of cotton, it made one quick dive to capture a meal in its talons. Again the wind stirred a bit with a few towering clouds gathering in the east. The day was changing.

"Sam, you gonna leave me hanging or do you just not want to talk about why you stopped preaching? Listen, if I am out of line in asking, just say so. Mostly I guess I'm just curious as to why you would spend all those years preparing for something and then just drop it."

Maybe Gary Lynn was reaching into untouchable territory, but what the heck. I had not seen him in three decades and probably would not see him again, so why not talk about the taboo subject. I figured if I had been such an influence on him, maybe he deserved an explanation.

"No, it's okay. I don' t mind talking about it. Seems like another lifetime, doesn't it? Had you ever met Sarah before today?"

"Don't guess I had. When your daddy passed away, I was in Vietnam. So we didn't cross then. I think that was about the only time you came back, wasn't it?"

"Yea, after that there just never seemed to be a reason. I never was much for that putting flowers on the grave and weeping over the tombstone. Don't mean to seem callous, but he was such a part of my life that I chose to remember him in other ways.

"You know, Sarah is a lawyer — a damn good one if I do say so. She was in law school when I was in the seminary, and we got out the same year. We talked about it a long time, and there was really no question that my ministry was more important to us than her lawyering so, like a lot of young preacher couples, we made the trek through country churches while trying to make ends meet in school.

"Then toward the end of law school, she got pregnant. We had a little son. Josh was his name. Cute little red-headed sucker, just like his daddy."

"I didn't know you had a son. I thought the twins were your only children. Where is Josh now?"

"Josh died on the night we both graduated from our graduate programs. He was 14 months old, Gary. It's a hard thing to talk about even after all these years."

Silence. Uncomfortable silence broken only by the search for words as Gary Lynn tried to make the appropriate response. "I'm sorry, Sam. Seems like I heard that, but I just forgot. Hey, maybe this is not the time to talk about all this."

"No, no. If you have the time, I probably need to talk about it. Sooner or later I'll get around to your question, just trying to give you a little background. Give me a few minutes and I'll circle back.

"After the shock of losing Josh, we just sort of drifted for a while. I got called to be the pastor of a church in Powderville, Texas. We spent a little over five years there.

That is where Kim and Karen were born. We had a pretty good run there. Built a new church, reached a lot of people. Maybe we did some good. I don't know, but I would like to think we did.

"Sarah got a job with the county attorney's office and I preached the Word. All in all, we were doing pretty good. But Gary, one day I couldn't do it anymore. You remember that sermon I preached for Rev. Moses' church? It was the second sermon I ever preached and that place was really rocking? You remember that?"

"Hell, I remember it. We went home from that service and in my father's country way he said, 'If that boy ain't got some nigger blood in him, his mama was sittin' close to one.' No offense to you or your mama or black people, but you know how people thought and talked back then. I'd give $100 right now to hear that sermon one more time."

I laughed, "Better watch out. You may not believe this, but I have a wire recording of it. After coming back on this trip, I may go have it transferred to tape if I can find someone to do that for me. I would kind of like to hear it again myself."

I went on, "There is no doubt in my mind that day was about the highlight of my preaching career. Old Moses had taught me about 'connectors' and 'vital phrases' and 'Say Amen!' and 'praise the Lord' stuff until it was coming out the top of my head. I preached some of that stuff one time in a seminary class and got the old Mississippi professor crying so much he gave me an A on the spot."

We both chuckled at the memory. It seemed to have caused Gary Lynn to have a momentary flashback too. We were enjoying the memory.

But it was time to move on to answering his question. "Gary, you remember how I got called to preach?"

"Something about Bro. Earl Lee and his gang coming to see you, wasn't it? You know, we were Methodists so we weren't real knowledgeable about how Baptists got their preachers. I just remember that one Sunday you were preaching, and if memory serves me right, pissing about every Sunday morning around 11 o'clock. Didn't miss preaching many Sundays all through high school, did you?"

"No, in fact I tended to do both on a pretty regular basis. Wish you hadn't brought that subject up. I still feel like I need to find two cars parked by a church every time I think about all that.

"But anyway, it took three years of high school under the guidance of our now-famous Bro. Earl Lee, Bro. Moses and — I have to admit — a little coaching from Leroy. I think about Leroy sometimes and all his dreams of being a great Methodist preacher. Then, what was he, 24 when he was killed in Nam?

"I spent four years of college at a great Baptist university, three years of graduate study in a wonderful seminary, and five years fighting the battles in a local church before I learned the greatest spiritual lesson of my life. I learned that you can't make it in that business on someone else's call. That make any sense to you?"

Gary Lynn reflected on that and said, "Probably not, but I don't have your history. What did it mean to you?"

"It meant that I found myself one night sitting in my den with a gun in my mouth ready to blow my brains out because I was doing something that I was not supposed to be doing."

He was stunned. "Sam, are you serious?"

"Man, I am as serious as death. As is common to say today, I could 'talk the talk,' but when it came to telling people to hear the voice of God, I just had never 'walked the walk.' I just became the master manipulator. You're not gonna believe this but just before I preached, I used to write down on a pad the number of people I was going to get down the aisle in the next service. About 90 percent of the time, I would nail it. Bro. Earl Lee had taught me the manipulation part pretty well. And it damn near got me killed."

About that time the Rogers' boy came back up the road still going about 70 miles an hour. This time he had a blonde on his arm and a cigarette in his mouth, driving with one arm around her and the other out the side window. Neither of us commented. We were into deeper territory.

Gary Lynn asked, "So, since you started telling this story, what did you do?"

"I walked away. Just couldn't do it anymore with any sense of moral integrity at all. The morning after the gun issue, Sarah and I sat down and talked about everything going on in my life. She had read me like a book and none of it came as a surprise. It had been years since I had a full night's sleep without taking some pill. She had seen it coming a long time before I had. She just didn't know how close I was to the edge.

"The next week I called a friend in Chicago and told him I needed a job. Funny, I met him in a revival where I was preaching and he came to know the Lord. He owned a big business in Oak Park, Illinois. He listened to my story and didn't give me any advice. Just suggested that Sarah and I catch the next plane to Chicago and spend a couple of days at his home with him and his wife.

"We left the twins with friends and flew up the next week. He had an opening in sales and, as he said, 'You sold me on Jesus, so you can probably use those same tactics to sell airplane parts. Come on up and we will work this out together.'

"Come next month, I will have been with the company almost 25 years. I'm now a corporate vice-president and run a division with more than 1,400 employees. Sarah joined a law firm in Chicago and has done really well. I am so proud of her. She does 'kind lawyering,' an oxymoron, I know. But she does. Sits on a couple of Fortune 100 boards. She is the real winner in the family. So all in all, God has been pretty good to us in spite of all the screw-ups at the beginning."

I stopped there thinking I had about covered the subject. But Gary Lynn, now concentrating on every word, continued to probe, "But what about your spiritual life. Sam, we laughed about it a little bit ago, but the fact is, you changed my life. I may have started out as a inch-deep Methodist, but today we are really involved in our church in Jonesboro. Sue and I have been at St. Andrew's Methodist Church for almost 20 years. It is just such a part of our lives.

"Can't say that we are fanatical about it, but we are there pretty much every Sunday. Hell, I even bake pancakes at the Men's Mission Breakfast every year. How could you just drop the church and walk away from it? Didn't any of that stuff you preached mean anything to you? It sure as hell had an influence on me."

"Gary, I never said I didn't believe it. I just said I was not called to preach it. Big difference. Didn't you say you taught history?"

"Yes."

"Ever study religious history in any depth?"

"Not a lot, but I could probably hold my own in a good conversation on the subject. Why?"

"Because I can explain what happened from a historical perspective better than I can from a contemporary one. Let me give it a shot.

"When Sarah and I first got to Chicago, we didn't jump back in a church for about four years. But we knew something was missing. So, like a lot of corporate ladder-climbing couples, we started bouncing around looking for a place that felt like home. Somehow we just didn't find Frostbite Baptist Church in Oak Park, Illinois. But the search went on with little to show for it.

"During those years, I spent a lot of time in spiritual depression, torn between being a success in business and yet feeling at odds with my earlier mission. I think — no, I know — I let the old elder tapes play in my head a lot. It was like Mama always said every time I talked to her, 'Son, do you think you will ever get back into the ministry?' As she got older, I called her two or three times a week. I don't think we ever talked that she didn't ask me that question."

Gary Lynn broke in with a chuckle, "That used to be the conversation at our house too. Wonder if old Sam is going to get back in the Lord's will? Heard it a hundred times over holiday dinner."

"Well, it was being discussed over dinner at our house too. During that respite from church, I wanted to believe in something. Shoot, I wanted to believe in God and getting saved and going to heaven and serving the Lord and all that stuff, but it just wasn't there. Never could get it to click.

"Then one day I was playing golf with one of my clients who was pretty active in an Anglican church near our house. Somehow we got on this subject and, just casually, he asked me if I had ever read the teachings of St. John of the Cross. I hadn't, so a few days later he sent me a book.

"In a nutshell, St. John of the Cross was a Spanish monk who lived around 1534. Really a spiritual mystic, he wrote about a lot of the stuff I was going through. There was one section I remember in great detail. He was writing about the often inability of man to connect with God. He used a phrase that just hit me between the eyes. He called this the great darkness of the soul. It is when we search and we do not find. We seek but we never connect. His message was this is an oftentrod road, but there *is* an end.

"The end comes when we empty ourselves and allow God to fill us.

"There is one of his writings that especially moved me, the Ascent of Mt. Carmel. In this work, he teaches the practice of loving attention to God. He encourages us to give up our memories and focus on what *can* be, not what was."

Realizing the length of my lesson, I halted, "Sorry, I get carried away sometimes."

By Gary Lynn was not ready to drop the subject. "No, I can see in your face this is something that is really important to you. But as one who has not had that struggle, I suppose my question has to do with this period of darkness. You mind telling me a little more about that?"

Seeing on Gary Lynn's face the same look I had seen in the mirror for many years, I pressed on, "Gary, it is the sadness of emptiness. It is always living in the shadow and never seeing the light. In my case, it was looking back and always searching for some outside sign that I was spiritually okay or that there was a ministry for me that was not pushed on me by old men of my youth. It was a terrible time, and I would not wish such a time on anyone."

The wind moved the branches of the willow. No one said anything for a few moments until finally Gary Lynn broke the silence. "Sam, this may sound strange, but I think I know what you mean. Maybe not to the depth you have known it, but I know. A few minutes ago, I talked about my church life as though it was pretty good. In my heart of hearts, I have to admit that making pancakes is about the peak of my spiritual life. Oh, we go to services. If you asked our pastor, he would say we are good members. But when you talk about the emptiness, I know what you are talking about. I guess I never called it the *darkness,* but I know what you are talking about just the same.

"Ever since we were in grade school I have gone to church, prayed over Sunday dinner, volunteered for the mission projects and pitched a few coins in the plate, but still, I do know the darkness you are talking about. Sometimes I lie in bed at night and just wonder what it would be like to experience God. You know what I mean?"

Did I ever. "Sure, I know. It comes from being so full of religion that we don't have time for God. I think that is what St. John of the Cross was saying. In my case I came to such a spiritual low right in the middle of doing so many spiritual things that I was ready to die to get relief. At that point, totally empty of everything, there was room for God."

I understood that this was new territory for Gary Lynn. But I sensed that he understood what I was talking about. His next statement affirmed that fact.

He looked up and there were tears in his eyes, "Sam, I'm in that darkness. How did you get out? I am so tired of doing religion that I will do anything to just know God. I'm ready for any advice you have to give."

It had been a long time since I had ministered to anyone at this level of intensity. But here was a man searching for light from one who said he had found it. Maybe God was asking me to put up or shut up.

I chose to move forward. "Gary, the only thing I know for certain is my own experience. It took me almost 20 years in the darkness before I walked into a church one day and found myself so low that only a Holy God could lift me up. So at that point, in my total emptiness, I asked Him to show me the light through the darkness and suddenly, in the deepest part of my soul, I knew that the light was beginning to burn again. I go back to St. John's writing. He writes about the need to empty one's self to the point where God can come in and fill the void. I was that empty at last.

"It was okay for me to not be a minister. It was okay for me to not pastor a church. It was okay for me to just rest in the hands of a loving God and find peace. All I had to do was ask for it. So at that moment, I asked and He answered, and for the past few years I have never known such spiritual peace.

"Maybe that is where you are. Maybe it is just time for you to let Him know you are as empty as you can be, but that you are ready to be filled by Him."

I looked at Gary Lynn as I was speaking and I could almost see his mind processing the words, not really knowing how to respond. Then he raised his face and looked directly into my eyes, "Sam, I am ready to do anything."

And before he could complete his thought we both heard his cell phone ringing. "Guess I'd better get that," he said as he got off the ground, ducked under the lower branches of the tree, and quickly made his way to his truck. I could not help overhearing, "Yea, just out here with Sam having a little talk. I'll be on home directly."

He put his phone back in his truck, stood there without moving for a minute, then walked back to the tree where I was now standing, brushing the dirt off my new suit pants. "Sam, it was good to talk to you, but I better run. Got a houseful over there and I'm supposed to be cooking for them tonight. Thanks for the talk. I'm glad things worked out for you. Guess I'll get things straight someday too."

We shook hands. There was an awkwardness to it that we both felt but did not acknowledge. It was as though a moment in time had been given to us and we allowed a silly cell phone to take it away.

Gary Lynn walked back to his truck without looking back. As he started the engine, he turned toward me and said, "Sam, maybe I'm not empty enough yet." And with that he backed into the road and drove away.

•••

I sat there a few minutes thinking about what had just taken place. I was disturbed by the discussion we had shared over the past hour. I knew what he would see in the mirror in the morning, and I wondered if he knew he had been as close to finding his spiritual self as I had been when I sat in that church those many years before.

He came so close, only to have it taken away by man's connection to the world: a cell phone.

Tomorrow he would try to forget our discussion. Tomorrow he would go out and try to do more, talk more, play the game of religion more, and he would pray that would bring him peace. But we both knew it would not.

In the past few years, I saw so many others in exactly the same spiritual perplexity that Gary Lynn was in. In all that time I saw only a handful actually make the leap from the darkness into the light. And today I was sad for all those who could not or would not make that leap.

By now the afternoon had slipped away and it was time to get back to my real world. The clouds had covered the sun and given a short respite from the heat. The hawk that had been witness to the day continued in wide circles above, lost in its own world of ascendancy toward the heavens.

I called Sarah and told her I would meet her at the church in about 30 minutes. She offered to come pick me up at the old homeplace, but I wanted to walk back into town one last time before we left for Chicago.

•••

As I made my way back to town, crossing Morgan's Creek along the way, I knew that I was at peace. I stopped on the bridge for a few moments. The water flowed slowly downstream with only an occasional ripple to break the reflection of the trees along its bank. I do not remember how long I stood just looking into the water, but it seemed to me like a rather long time.

During those quiet moments, it dawned on me that I was really at peace with God and with myself. I had come back to the place where this journey into hell and back had started. I had come home to Frostbite, Arkansas, faced my demons, and I had survived.

But most of all I realized that this God who had filled all the dark places had allowed me to experience these things from the past without any regret.

Excerpt

from Ben Gill's forthcoming novel
The Journal
anticipated release date 2004

My name is Daniel Ellis and for 39 years I held the distinguished position as head of the Waldon Institute in London. Emanuel Waldon, a man of great wealth and intellectual curiosity, established the Waldon Institute in 1903. The Institute was his legacy, the recipient of his entire estate at the time of his death. Its purpose, simply stated, was to disprove the foundation of faith upon which the Christian religion was established.

An atheist by proclamation, Mr. Waldon's entire focus was to prove the fallacy of misplaced faith in the Christ of the Bible. What fueled this mission is yet unknown to me. But what is known is that upon his death in 1919 the Institute was endowed with funds that would assure its continued search for information that would discredit the largest religious following of mankind — the great body of humanity who call themselves "Christians." I am pleased to say that, through the saving grace of a loving God, I too am numbered among that body. Therefore, even as I write this today, I do so with a great deal of amazement at the turn in life's road that so impacted my life many years ago.

That turn came as a result of a totally unsolicited approach received by me at a time when my own career as a Biblical scholar was first blooming into some lofty status among the Christian community. In the spring of 1960 a committee of the Waldon Institute's Board of Directors approached me. It was told to me sometime later that I was brought to their attention after the publication of my second manuscript, "Faith — The Foundation for Followship." As Chairman of the Department of Biblical studies at Lanford University in Chicago, I had published this book and with its publication had received a certain amount of acclaim as the "defender of the faith" at a time in the nation's history when the faith definitely needed defending.

"God is Dead" was the cover story of TIME magazine and a cynical young generation had decided to place their faith in the pipe of the Timothy Learys of academia rather than in the traditions of religious belief that had sustained the generations that preceded them. My self-chosen profession of "defender" came with the territory of my position rather than from some deep-seated internal grounding in the faith.

So it was with some receptivity that I entertained the first thoughts of accepting the position as Executive Director of the Waldon Institute. I had remained in my office for a number of student conferences, most of which would likely be long forgotten by my theologically shallow students. Late in the afternoon when the sun was early wasted behind the cloudy curtain of the winter sky, some vague vagabond of the mail room came by to deliver the letter that would change my life and the direction of my career. The exploration letter sent by Mr. George Williams, Chairman of the Board of the Institute, was rather straightforward and intellectually challenging.

Waldon Institute
One Leesworth Road
South Kensington Place
London
March 3, 1960

Dear Dr. Ellis:

My name is George Williams and I am the Chairman of the Board of Directors of the Waldon Institute in London. As you may be aware our distinguished Executive Director for these past twenty years, Dr. William Thompson, was recently stricken with a heart attack and subsequently passed away.

Dr. Thompson had led the research of the Institute in its search to fulfill the mission of the Institute with great zeal and vigor. He shared the beliefs of our founder, Mr. Emanuel Waldon, and spent a great deal of his life searching for the documentation that we believe will ultimately indicate that the Christ figure in history was little more than a story that got out of hand in its telling over these past centuries.

We, the Board of Directors, are well-aware of your standing within the Christian community. We have been impressed with your defense of the "faith" and would now ask you to consider putting your theories to the test? As strange as you might find this offer to be, we would propose that you consider accepting the position left open by the death of our beloved colleague, Dr. Thompson.

If you truly believe in the Christian view of Biblical history, and certainly we have no doubt that you are sincere in your beliefs, we would like to offer you a position through which you can either prove or disprove that view. We can certainly offer you a position that will secure your financial future and that of your family forever. So from a purely selfish standpoint we believe you will find our offer worth exploring.

However, even more stimulating should be the opportunity to be supported by unlimited funds to find a basis for your belief and the beliefs of millions of others. In the vernacular of your country, we are offering you the opportunity to "put up or shut up" and we are willing to fund the process.

As you may know, our Institute has a research staff unmatched in academia. In the search to disprove the Christian myth, we have funded literally hundreds of archeological expeditions in the Middle East or, as you might prefer, the "Holy Land." However, in every case, our teams have entered into the process with a bias of finding proof that there is neither basis for nor substance in the belief of Jesus as Messiah. To this point, these years of expedition have neither proven nor disproved our premise.

Therefore, it is the desire of our Board to enlist the services of someone from the other side. Rather than approaching the subject to disprove the myth it is now our desire to enlist the services of a true believer and ask that person to lead our Institute in finding proof that Christ was, indeed, everything the Christians say he was. The objective will then change from one of disproving the faith to one of proving the existence and validity of Jesus as the Son of God.

Obviously, your credentials are impeccable in this regard. Your writings and status in the Christian community give you the platform and the visibility we seek in our next Executive Director. We are willing to fund, in any manner you might chose, the search for the truth in this matter. Prove the Christ and therefore encourage the faith or find proof of the mere humanity of a personality in history whose status would be no more or less than any other cult leader. The only stipulation will be that when and if your findings are rendered, you will publish them with the full backing of the Institute.

Lest there be some confusion as to our purpose let me simply state it. Our purpose is to provide you the tools to find the truth in this matter. Since we believe the truth will support our belief, we are coming to you to carry us to the conclusions of our search. However, if we are correct, and we do trust your integrity as a Biblical researcher, we would expect you to go before the world and represent the Institute in proclaiming the fact that you, along with millions before you, are indeed simply following a master manipulator. This man called Jesus.

I suppose the question is simply this. Do you believe in your faith enough to seek scientific proof rather than some nebulous supernatural faith? If so, join us in the search and accept and proclaim the truth whatever that truth may bring.

We will give you a few weeks to consider these matters and then I will contact you again later in the month. I do have a trip planned to Chicago within the next six weeks and would enjoy the opportunity to discuss these matters with you.

Sincerely,
George Williams
Chairman

Thus began my association with the Institute.

03033